DERBY ACADEMY

1 7 8 4

2023 BOOK AWARD

Through Their Lenses

Award-Winning Short Stories by Tweens

Lune Spark Books, Apex, NC

Publisher: Lune Spark LLC

PO Box 1443, Morrisville, NC, 27560, United States

www.lunespark.com

Young Writers' Resources: www.lunespark.com/youngwriters

Email: books@lunespark.com

Phone: +1 (919) 809-4235

Hardback ISBN 13: 978-1-947960-42-8
Paperback ISBN 13: 978-1-947960-41-1
eBook ISBN 13: 978-1-947960-43-5

Cover art by Mitali Mishra

1. Short stories 2. Anthology 3. Creative writing 4. Young writers

First edition

To the young writers who have the courage to tell their stories.

"Start writing, no matter what. The water does not flow until the faucet is turned on."
— Louis L'Amour"

Introduction

When I started the Lune Spark Short Story Contest in 2017, I did not really know what to expect. I had just one goal: to provide a platform for young writers to get discovered and find readers for their stories. I'm very pleased that as of this writing, the contest has entered its fourth year and has acquired a reputation as being one of the best contests in the world for young writers!

I'm also very proud to say that over the past couple of years many of our previous contestants have let me know that this contest worked as a stepping stone toward their goal of becoming a writer. Some of these young writers have successfully released their first novels. So if you know a young writer, please let him/her know about the contest by passing on the website:

lunespark.com/youngwriters

The impact this contest is making in bringing new young writers to the world is becoming more apparent with each year—and that's the biggest reward I can ever expect for all the time I spend every year running this contest.

Just like in past years, the stories this year encompass a tremendous amount of creativity and imagination. I feel proud to introduce yet another excellent anthology of stories by talented young writers.

My special gratitude goes to the following people. Running the contest and publishing this book couldn't have been possible without their help!

- The participants of the 2020 Lune Spark Short Story Contest and their parents for their high degree of engagement, enthusiasm, and support.
- The judges of the 2020 contest: Alexandra Hubbell, Osman Welela, SF Benson, Tamara Burross Grisanti, and Vikas Khair. Alexandra Hubbell and SF Benson helped us last year as well—their continued commitment to this cause is highly commendable!

Lastly, the best gift to a writer is a review. So let your take on their stories reach them in the form of a review anywhere you like—on a book website or on your blog. Rest assured that they will very eagerly be reading every single review, looking for encouragement and constructive criticism. Happy reading!

—Pawan Mishra, Apex, North Carolina
January 2021

Contents

Diary of a Dying Soldier
Raphaël Courouble

Tired. Exhausted. My body was drained. As I walked through the muddy landscape, I was drenched with sweat, and I could not open my mouth. While all the others were asking to rest, I did not say a word. Why? I could not say. Exasperated, I marched silently, with my heavy shoes filled with sand. I could not hear the birds singing around me. I could not hear the ditties my companions were singing. I was deaf. Not only were my ears deaf, but also my heart. I could not close my eyes without crying. I could not open them without feeling ruthless and merciless.

The feeling trapping me was maybe the most intense a human could go through: shame. This bitter dishonor made me feel at the mercy of my feelings and unworthy of God. As I walked through the dust, through the mud, through my pain, I was wondering who I was and what I was doing in this world immensely far from any peaceful region. I once had a family who cared about me. Yet I had refused to stay with them and had preferred to go into the midst of action. I had chosen to join the army.

My first days were harsh, but I felt in my element. We were trained for days and days that quickly transformed into weeks, which transformed into months. Life was quite peaceful. My companions and I played games, and we rarely had any missions. That is if you don't count arresting smugglers. We sometimes had to camp in the middle of nowhere to train, and that was something I loved. You could light up a small fire in the grass. Not only could owls be heard, but also wolves in search of a meal that could fill their empty stomachs in the middle of an immensely cold night that could make my blood shiver with fear and excitement.

One day, my first real mission came. Although our country had nothing to do with it, we were required to interfere in the Persian Gulf. We were less than a hundred. It was during

9

the Arab Spring. Word spread that the police were having trouble. I did not know who to support. The media's perspective changed every day, and people on social networks had mixed feelings about it. I never really understood why we meddled with all those people's lives. Some said it was for our country to have petrol, and others said it was to help their local authorities. I had uneasy thoughts about it, but I did what I was told. Before I left, I went to see my family one last time. Oh, how I remember their anxious and mournful faces. How I remember my old father's last words to me:

"I have always been very proud of you, son, and I will always be with you in the battlefield. I will be in your heart. Good luck, son."

How I missed him. He had been so worried when I left. After losing my mother, he could not lose anyone else. Not now at least. He had strived to keep me alive, and although his words seemed calm, his heart was not. How I admired him. As far as I knew, he could have died by this point and joined my dear mother.

I missed her every day. She was a brilliant scientist who had died when one of her experiments turned out to be dangerous and blew up her laboratory. Would she be proud of me, if she saw a brave soldier standing on her doorstep?

Nevertheless, as months had passed, I had become violent, and I started not to know who I was or why I was here. I had wanted a thrilling adventure, which I had received. But within a few days of our mission, the worst had happened.

Those sickening memories distinctly came back to me while walking through the dusty landscape. I remembered my wife. She was sorrowful when I left her. I also remember the last time I saw her. She had her beautiful green dress on and was standing among cherry and magnolia trees, and near her, a dove was carrying a rose—not an olive branch like you would imagine. A pinkish-red rose with some blots of light orange.

We had met for the first time five years ago; we were young and innocent then. Having recently finished our studies, we were both seeking jobs. She was very compassionate, yet that did not prevent her from often losing her temper and being in a bad mood. Still, she truly was caring and gentle. Due to all the good recollections I had gained from being with her, I sometimes wished I could forget her, so it would not cause me so much pain. Yet every day, whatever my mood was, I wrote her a letter. It was my only source of joy. Had she, alas, also forgotten me? If not for her, I would not be alive. If not for her, life would not be worth enduring.

As my regiment was marching with uneasy feelings, I remembered what had happened next. I had killed a man. The demonstrations in the busy roads were becoming more intense. Our regiment was pushing forward, and rocks were thrown at us. Shields could not protect us. We first replied by kicking people away, but most of us were pushed to the ground. One of my best friends collapsed. The chaos had only begun. We tried to stop them, but this very same chaos that had erupted would not be blocked; and as the tension grew, bullets were shot unpredictably in every direction. Then I killed a furious man in the crowd. I looked him in the eye, and I killed him. I had killed a man, not knowing who he was. It was too late. The bullet was fired...

Why did we get involved in this when it wasn't our country's responsibility? Why did I leave my loving family? How did I let myself participate in a merciless, bloody struggle? How could I have imagined it would be anything like that?

My history teacher in school—it seemed so long ago, so distant from now—had talked to us for hours on end about some of the cruelest wars in history. And I had been bored to death. So many times I had drawn during lessons and joked about the subject. War? Were there any? Had the word ever existed? I had thought that they were ancient and that horrors like those did not exist anymore.

I was wrong.

Wars nowadays were just as, if not more, cruel. Be that as it may, now nothing mattered. I could not go home. I killed a man. The only way to end my pain was by dying.

I stopped walking, took out my gun, and without a word, let a second pass. It was the longest second I ever knew. Memories crossed my brain, and a tear rolled down my cheek. One single tear. Why was I lamenting my fate? I knew I had to do this, but could I? Had I the strength or was I weak? Weak as I had been before. Weak of my emotions and of my fate. Yet, as if life did not want me to die, a voice in my head told me not to. It was becoming stronger, and it took control of all my emotions. Then I saw my mother. I could not tell you how. Nor did I want to know how. For explanation, I admitted that my head, which had suffered enough atrocities, was becoming mad: I was delirious. War had changed all of us. Maybe it was actually one of my companions. I do not know. I heard her speak in her usual protective voice:

"My son, I gave birth to you, I cherished you and helped you, so don't do that, my son, please, I beg you. If not for yours, then for my sake. Every life has its difficulties, but you are meant to overcome them. Please, my son..."

It was too late. A bullet was fired...

Ring Bestowed

Eunice Lee

I stepped out of my car and locked it. Taking a deep breath in, I looked around me. There were plush green trees, a small gently flowing river, and a small cottage in the distance. When I was younger, I had vowed to buy it, but I never did. I never really had a reason to.

The sky was mostly clear with just a couple of clouds. Views like this always managed to calm me down. Since I run my own company, work can be pretty stressful sometimes. This place is my sanctuary. It's also where I come when I have conflicts in my personal life. I've had this place all my life; it's one of the only places that brought happy memories to me from when I was a child. My mother always seemed different here, almost like she cared.

Of course she cared, Aubrey. She gave you the ring, remember? How could you say such a thing! I thought.

"Mom, why does my life have to be so...so hard?" I asked.

Kneeling in front of my mother's tombstone, I picked at the grass around me and continued speaking, "It seems like everyone is leaving me, and it's all because of me… Dave broke up with me, three years all gone down the drain."

I covered my eyes with my hand and sobbed. I never cried this hard before, but Dave, my ex, reminded me of my mom a lot, and while that sounds slightly weird, it isn't. I did love him a lot, but at first, I went out with him because I thought that I could right all the wrongs that I had with my mom. Stupid, I know. Turns out I was getting in the way of his career, so we broke up. Or to put it more plainly: he left me.

As my sobs faded to silent tears, I twisted my ring that my mother gave to me. It's a peculiar habit of mine, but it does help. The ring was originally my great-great-grandmother's, and it became a tradition for the ring to be passed down to a daughter in every generation, right before the girl's wedding day or the day her mother passed away. The ring was a symbol of peace and success; it had always been known that the ring brought the wearer luck and peace. It kind of worked like a talisman.

It certainly seemed to work; I am descended from a line of successful, wealthy women. It's heartwarming that, despite all of the conflicts we had, my mother would still want to wish wealth, success, and love for me. Even if the love part never seems to work out.

It's okay, Aubrey, I reassured myself.

I sighed deeply and slowly stood up, brushing the leaves off my suit. I wanted to pick some roses for my mom before leaving. Roses were her favorite flowers—I found that out from my grandmother. I called her "Nana" because supposedly "Grandma" made her sound really old.

Nana was always there for me. For my whole life, my mother had never been around much. She always had to work. She had a dream to become the youngest woman billionaire, and she pursued it ferociously. So, naturally, Nana took care of me. She was like the mother I never had, but I would never admit that out loud, because that would be betraying my mother somehow. After all, she did care for me a lot; she had given me the ring for crying out loud!

"Ouch," I exclaimed when I accidentally pricked my finger on a thorn. I sucked on it, trying to reduce the blood flow, and picked up the rose with my other hand, careful not to prick myself again, and walked back toward her tombstone.

I carefully laid the rose in front of the tombstone, right in front of the engraved words, "In loving memory of Rose Hilton, beloved daughter and wife."

What bothered me the most was that there was no "mother" part. Nana said that it was because they ran out of space, but that probably isn't true.

No, don't think that. Stupid Aubrey, mother gave you the ring, remember? I reminded myself.

I sighed again, sat back down, and started to stroke the grass around me carefully.

Ring, ring.

There goes my phone, ruining my moment, I thought. I let it ring for a few more seconds before picking it up.

"What do you want?" I asked, thinking it was another one of my incompetent employees again.

"Hello, is this Aubrey Hilton?" a strange voice asked.

"Yes, it is," I cautiously replied.

"I am sorry to inform you that your grandmother, Lily Hilton, is in the Goldenbridge Hospital due to a heart attack."

My phone slid out of my hands. *Nana is at the hospital because of a heart attack? Nana is at the hospital, my Nana.*

I ran back to the car and raced to the hospital in a blur.

"Aubrey Hilton?" the hospital receptionist called after I had checked in.

I slowly stood up and walked toward her. Immediately, she ushered me into the private room that Nana was in.

As soon as I walked in, I saw Nana lying on the bed, connected to a bunch of IVs and a heart monitor. I was trying hard not to cry because I had to be strong for her. I told Nana that she was going to be okay and tried to reassure her a bit more, but she said she knew her time was almost up.

Nana asked me to do her one last favor. She asked me if she could wear the ring one last time. The ring was really special to all of us, but Nana in particular because it was her engagement ring. My grandfather passed a while back, and it really took a toll on us, but especially Nana. According to the stories that Nana told, my grandfather was a really sweet man. He supposedly bought Nana an engagement/promise ring, but he knew how much our ring meant to her, so he asked my great-grandmother if he could propose with it.

I slowly took it off and put it on my palm, gesturing for her to take it.

She gingerly picked it up from my palm and inspected it slowly, something I had never done.

Then Nana asked, "Honey, what ring is this? It looks a lot like the real ring, but the setting is different. In fact, the stone is different too."

Slightly amused, I told her that of course it was the ring that mother gave me, the ring that got passed down for six generations and counting, the ring that guaranteed money, success, and love.

Then she said the words that I would remember for the rest of my life, "Darling, that's not the ring."

I sat on the waiting room chair while massaging my temples. The words "darling, that's not the ring" replayed in my head, almost like a mantra. The look of pity that Nana gave me was just infuriating. I'm not some broken girl whose mother never cared about her.

I let out a small sob and clutched my head. The tears kept streaming down. Once the tears had slowed, I pulled my hand up and inspected the ring, wanting to make sure before jumping to a conclusion.

Nana is pretty old. She might have forgotten what the ring feels like.

The ring was fake, I thought as realization dawned across my face. *Nana wasn't lying. In fact, my mom was the one who lied.*

If you looked closely, you could see that there were little cracks alongside the supposed "diamond." It looked like cheap plastic. If you looked at the actual band, you could see that it wasn't actual silver, it was cheap metal that was starting to tarnish with specks of orange and green.

So this is what I meant to my mother, I thought bitterly.

It never really was me, was it? It was always my mother's expectations and dreams. She valued her business deals over me, she never understood the meaning of love, and she always thought that I was holding her back from her dreams. Which is kind of funny because I always stayed with Nana. It was her own fault that she never made the "first women billionaire" title.

All of these years, I'd felt so much pressure to live a perfect life. To have wealth, success, and love, like the women who had worn the ring before me.

I silently slid the ring off my finger and pressed my foot against the mechanic peddle that opened the trash can, and I tossed it in. Without looking back, I silently walked away.

Strangely enough, after a long, long time, I finally felt free.

Script Climate Change Magic
Nico Roman Cordonier Gehring

"As the morning sun rose over the shattered stone shores and flooded fens of East Anglia, the boy swam powerfully inland toward his brave, ragged band of friends, grimly determined to rebuild after the devastation, and to ensure that such a climate crisis would never happen again," concluded the narrator in a clear, fierce, yet hopeful tone.

Tears in their eyes, the audience stood to applaud, their shadows reaching to fill the garden pavilion. As one, the Guerilla Theater Troupe actors stepped forward, bowed, and then turned with their own special applause to the young playwright, who wheeled his chair forward to accept their standing ovation, stage torches gleaming over his ebony face and long, graceful hands.

Story had never anticipated such success. His first plays were edgy, difficult, consumed by the youth of the climate-strikes protest movements for whom they had first been penned. He wrote them out longhand in loose-leaf notebooks, quietly curled in the corner of a battered, worn-down public library and bound them into his folios.

Sometimes, though, on quiet nights, new dramas would demand to be written, to be spoken and heard, to change hearts and minds. Story would set aside his usual pencils and take up his secret pen, the one with indigo ink that he had received as a gift from a famous playwright, years before, in London's Globe theater, just after the fire that had taken his legs. In these stolen moments, dramas would crystallize into script, flowing through Story's soul, forcing their way out onto rough lined pages, into the narratives of his actors, and from there, into the ever-changing lives and myriad potential futures of his rapt social-movement-participating audiences.

Story's work began during the first-ever climate strike organized by the youth of his city. Children and youth from many schools had gathered to raise their voices against the policies and decisions that were, according to scientists, risking their very futures. After the speeches by eco-council student leaders, a group of twelve children climbed up the steps of Shire Hall and called out the first lines of an inspiring chant. Thousands of voices, young but resolute, echoed back their cry. The children's dramatic chant raised the energy of the crowd, building their commitment with their cries. Story, with his young face and voice in his tiny wheelchair, joined them, fascinated. After the march, he circled the rapidly dispersing crowd until he found the eco-council's young Guerilla Theater performers. After congratulating them, he asked if they might need a playwright, transcribing new scripts for their climate strikes. The band of children, who had only just formed their troupe, agreed enthusiastically.

His first indigo ink play was for a climate strike in a small town on the fringes of a dark, beautiful moss-shrouded oak forest. One spring, in Story's drama, the watershed authorities and council authorities agreed on a terrible plan to degrade the historic forests, paving the way for investments in grim new asphalt roads, cold chrome high-rises, and obsidian office buildings. As Guerilla Theater performed, the youth discovered the plans and rose up, restoring every glade of the historic forest, creating new nature reserves, and foiling the plot, as they protected the solemn, precious, ancient emerald groves and unique wildlife surrounding their home.

Story's second indigo play was performed in the summer, revealing collusion between water companies and river authorities, destroying the flow of their vital river, drying up the sapphire waters of the natural chalk streams in order to overdevelop infrastructure for expensive, water-inefficient subdivisions. As the Guerilla Theater presented Story's drama, a network of student activists mobilized to defend the last wild waterways, joining with scientists and adult conservationists to restore the chalk streams, recover their shimmering riparian riverside eco-systems, and prompt the resignation of the water company CEO alongside adoption of new laws to protect their precious watercourses. The students cheered as their coalition gathered thousands of supporters, their petition collected millions of signatures, and their rushing rivers and fenlands were saved.

In Story's third play, which began in the autumn, a boy street artist spray-painted startling scenes of desperate endangered animals being forced out of their habitats by a large corporation whose profits were more important than nature or values. Through the messages in his marvelous, multicolored magical murals, the citizens gained awareness, and the corrupt council was overcome. As Guerilla Theater performed Story's play, beautiful, vibrant, meaningful murals mysteriously appeared throughout the city hosting their performance, and a new public movement won the inspiration and hope to finally indict the corrupt mayor and the bankrupted, disgraced firm. The boy street artist, seldom seen, faded out of existence until needed again.

As the Guerilla Theater Troupe continued to meet and perform during climate strikes, Story wrote faster and more furiously. The special indigo dramas swirled onto his pages, into the scripts of performers, and into the lives and futures of the youth. However, Story also listened and learned about the dangers of climate change. He saw the science reports and maps illuminating that if greenhouse gas emissions could not be stopped, keeping the temperature rise below 1.5 degrees, and resilience could not be secured, the floodwaters would rise, and storm surges would risk drowning his own little town on the East Anglia coastline, alongside many other vulnerable areas around the world.

Indeed, that very winter, the storms became wilder, angrier, and hungrier. They lashed against the harbors and the paltry flood defenses of Story's fragile seaside town, and then, in one particularly violent hurricane, broke through.

In his wheelchair, Story could not run across the flooded, uneven ground. He was left behind in the evacuation. He waited for help, but none came.

Instead, he received a frantic call from his own troupe, trapped in the old brick library with the children from their at-risk kids theater workshop.

As the waters rose outside his little room, new dramas—entrances, action sequences, dialogues—all whirled and shrieked, crying out to be written. Story raised his indigo ink pen. Into this last play, the most powerful he could ever write, Story poured his own soul.

For although Story had been trapped in his chair for a very, very long time, with legs that could not support him, he had always been able to swim...

In his indigo ink, the drama of transformation wrote itself, supported by special effects and stage directions for a boy playwright with a powerful dolphin tail.

In his winter play, Story leaped courageously into the rushing storm waves and swam rapidly to the terrified children, held barely above the dark, angry floodwaters by exhausted Guerilla Theater youth. He had been searching the ferocious sea-over-land for hours, and the children, screaming as their makeshift barriers collapsed and as the waters broke through the windows of their tiny public library refuge, were already sinking into the glowing gloom.

He had only seconds to reach them before they might be lost forever. He would risk his life to safe theirs, just as his theater troupe had valiantly performed his plays, saving town after town from the terrible impacts of climate change advancing across the land.

Story spotted the blackened oak desks to which the children had been desperately clinging, but they were already gone, sinking into the murky, dangerous, violent waters that grasped and clawed at each stroke of his daring tail. Story took a deep breath and bravely dived.

21

As a shout of joy rung out, the first small heads emerged. Seconds later, Story, carrying two children and towing one of his brave actors, stroked furiously for the library rafters, lifting the children to safety. Scarcely had he secured the first little ones when he was diving back, pulling more children upward with the help of his tired, courageous Guerilla Theater players. Soon, the children rested in the high beams of the library, feet on the dark wood of the tall bookshelves above the highest windows, as the storm surge slowly began to recede. They tried to thank Story, but he swam onward, determined to save other lives.

At the end of the long night, having rescued hundreds of residents from the worst natural disaster to assault the coast of England in hundreds of years, Story leaned quietly against the soft gray stones of a former high-rise building, now a small island. He was already filling his special pen with indigo ink for a new ending to his greatest, most powerful play.

In Story's new ending, political and corporate decision-makers woke up after the storms and recognized their responsibility for the climate emergency, declaring that their destructive policies would end. They reworked their science, their systems, and their budgets, adopting and enforcing new laws and policies on climate change and disaster risk reduction, worldwide, and steering all new finance and investments toward carbon negative initiatives. Basically, they finally enacted the profound climate contributions that they had been promising for years.

In Story's indigo ink script, as predawn rays illuminated the battered library, the youth from Story's Guerilla Theater Troupe struggled awake. They passed the salvaged children to desperate, relieved parents, then staggered down to the sea, seeking their lost playwright friend. As their county, their country, and their world awoke to a new day, the boy's powerful dolphin tail faded, its magic no longer needed.

The narrator took center stage, and the glowing torches illuminated her fierce, hopeful, and dramatic declaration: "As the morning sun rose over the shattered stone shores and flooded fens of East Anglia, the boy swam inland toward his brave, ragged band of friends, grimly determined to rebuild after the devastation, and to ensure that such a climate crisis would never happen again..,"

The Boy Who Loved Peanut Butter Waffles

Brady Hammond

Meet Jack. He's in first grade. He loves peanut butter waffles.

Here's how to make them. Toast a waffle until crispy. Not too crispy. It should be slightly brown. Let the waffle sit one minute on a plate to cool. Otherwise pack your bag for Drip City come topping time.

Slather peanut butter (Jack likes extra crunchy) on half of the waffle. No need to be perfect. Cut the waffle down the middle. Lay one half on top of the other to make a sandwich. Voilà!

Jack eats peanut butter waffles almost every morning for breakfast. If he doesn't eat one in the morning, he eats it for lunch or after school or with dinner.

Sometimes Jack eats three peanut butter waffles a day. True story.

While eating a peanut butter waffle one Sunday, Jack got news.

"You're gonna be a big brother, fella," Dad said. Mom smiled big. This was big. Good big? Jack was unsure. The situation was messier than Jack's messiest waffle.

Too soon after, out popped Fester, Jack's baby brother.

Fester cried. A lot. When he met Jack, Fester fussed more. Then he sneezed, turned beet red, and swelled to the size of Australia.

Was Fester sick? Doctor Alan would know. "According to the tests, little Fester is fuming because he has allergies. They're not to his brother. Nuts are to blame.

"Nuts!" Jack screamed. "I love peanut butter. I hate my brother!"

While Jack was at school, his mom cleaned out the cabinets. She put all the extra crunchy peanut butter, smooth peanut butter, almond butter, unicorn and hazelnut butter (the list continues) in a box in the pantry.

Jack's mom sealed it with six layers of duct tape and a sign that read, "KEEP OUT!" It sat on the tippy-top shelf in no-man's-land.

Now Jack fumed.

Jack emptied all $11.72 cents from his piggy bank to buy two top secret jars of peanut butter. Too bad Jack's dad intercepted the goods like a linebacker ready to sack. Goodbye, victory. Hello, timeout.

The next day, Jack made a playdate at his friend Larry's house. That's Larry "Granola Bar" Goodwin, if you're curious. He's got every kind of bar stocked at the ready. Bummer that Jack's mom had schooled Mrs. Goodwin to hide anything with nuts from hungry Jack.

Meanwhile, Jack's parents had been taking Fester to allergy specialists. Only time would tell if Fester would ever be able to tolerate peanut butter and everything else Jack craved.

Then Doctor Alan had news.

Jack could eat peanut butter out of the house when Fester was six months old, as long as Jack brushed his teeth and washed his hands right after. Jack agreed. "I'll do it whatever it takes to keep little Pester, er Fester, safe."

The funny thing was, Jack stopped caring much about peanut butter. He realized Fester was kinda cute, even fun in his own Festery way.

Rather than wake each morning wanting a peanut butter waffle, Jack wondered what tricks his little bro was mastering. Besides waffles with butter and jam weren't so bad after all.

It turns out brothers are better than food.

Of course, it is pretty awesome when Fester isn't around and big brother can eat whatever he wants and play whatever he wants and watch whatever he wants, maybe all at the same time with peanut butter in the mix. But Jack's teeth have never been whiter from all that brushing after peanut butter.

Blackout
Sachin Chandran

July 12, 2910 was… WHOA, sorry it was 2019 not 2910! Anyway, July 12, 2019 was a dark day, literally. There was a blackout across the whole world. It was three hours long, and no one was really harmed by it. Well, except for one person…

Zeek Edmonds V was an ordinary fifteen-year-old. He had a B average in school and was of average height with brown hair and freckles. He looked normal and talked normally, and usually this is the point where I tell you he was actually a crime fighting vigilante or something, but nope. He was the most average teenager you could find.

All of this changed when the blackout happened. Zeek somehow got transported to 1906, and his world was shaken.

Zeek had just gotten up from his plain white bed, in his plain white pajamas in his plain white room...you get the point. He was pretty plain. Anyway, I'm getting off track. He headed down to his bathroom to brush his teeth. He picked up his brush from the white counter and brushed with his flavorless toothpaste. He then picked up his floss and started flossing. As he was about to finish, it happened. Everything went dark in the world. Zeek started to feel a bit queasy. He then fell to the floor and vanished without a trace.

Zeek didn't know where he was and more importantly when he was. All he knew was that this was not his home. It looked so old and primitive. All the houses were made of brick, and he could smell some burning wherever he went. Zeek was lost like a butterfly that was separated from its swarm. He saw someone in a horse-drawn carriage and tried his best to flag them over. The driver noticed him and pulled over.

Zeek then asked, "What day is it?" to which the driver responded, "Why, it's April 18, 1906 of course. The bigger question is about your clothes."

Lots of thoughts were racing through Zeek's head at this moment. This had to be a practical joke, right? Also the date struck a significance in his mind, though he could not place it. He turned around to question the driver some more, but he had sped off into the distance leaving only dust behind.

Zeek was now in a predicament. He didn't know where he was or who he could talk to. This didn't look like home, but something felt very familiar about this place. He tried to find clues to know where he was. He walked for what seemed like an hour until he saw it. The oldest and best shop in his city, Marcini's Sandwiches. He always went there after school with his friends. He was in San Francisco. The one upside to this situation was that he knew how to navigate through this city because he lived there. The problem was he knew what was about to happen. Too bad that it was too late.

The earth started to shake hard and jarringly. Everybody around Zeek was panicking, and you have probably figured out why. Zeek was running around trying to find a place to duck down into. All the buildings around him were crumbling down. It felt as if the world was ending. It felt like Earth was getting crushed in a mortar and pestle. He found a bench and dove under it, hanging on for dear life. He was panicking, felt very helpless, and vulnerable during this one minute of his life.

Zeek was repeating to himself the same words over and over again through tears that showed what it was like to be truly afraid: "Help me, please, somebody make this stop." Although he knew no one could help, he kept on saying those words, as if they were his only hope. He didn't know what to do or if he would live. That was the scariest part of it all. Not knowing whether you are going to be alive after it is all over is terrifying. But all of a sudden, the earth stopped shaking, and there was a sickening moment of silence. This was obviously interrupted by more screaming. Zeek came up from underneath that bench to see what all the commotion was. After all, the earthquake was over, and he didn't see a reason to panic. That was until he got up and saw it.

His skin felt like it was being grilled over hot coals. Everything around him was engulfed in flames. This was what he had forgotten about this day. He remembered in that moment what his fourth-grade teacher had told him. *It wasn't the earthquake that did the most damage. It was the fires afterward.*

He recalled her telling the class about how when the earthquake happened, the stoves, which were powered by fire, fell over, making everything burn up.

He ran around, using his shirt as a mask to stop the smoke from going into his lungs. He wanted to find somewhere to hide and cower while other people were suffering. If he survived, he felt like he would create so many more generations of people in the future, and because of that, he was being selfless in a way.

He found the perfect safe zone. A depression in the dirt large enough to hold him. He was going to go in and cover himself with dirt so he wouldn't burn up. He was about to make it when he heard a noise, a noise that would change his life forever.

He turned around and saw a baby and mother trapped in their home that was quickly turning to ash. It was then that he wondered if he should go in and get them out. He was torn between saving his own life or risking himself to save two others. His mind said save yourself, but his gut said save them. In the end he went right in front of the house and did the uncommon thing for once in his life. He ran straight into the house and right through the flames.

Zeek finally knew how brisket felt. His skin was popping with blisters and his eyes were watering like Niagara. He wanted to get out and jump into the bay, but he knew he couldn't. He had to help those two people get out. As he was running up the stairs, he heard them clearly. He then rounded the corner and saw them. Ash covered their faces and their burned clothes. He could tell they were fighting for their lives. They were trapped by flaming wreckage. Zeek scanned the situation and found an opening that was barely large enough for them.

He looked through the hole and yelled to the family, "Come with me!" He wasn't sure they heard him, but they got the message and followed him through. He rushed through the halls and down the stairs pounding on the cracked and burned floors. He motioned the family to follow him and go faster. They finally made it to the front of the house. Zeek ran toward the door with the family but was stopped by falling debris.

The rubble was blocking their way, but there was a hole that was barely big enough for the two people that he was rescuing. He motioned them to the hole, and they made it through by the skin of their teeth.

At this point, the house was crumbling like pastry under a knife. He knew what was about to happen, and he knew he couldn't change his fate. But he had changed theirs. The two people jumped onto the street. Zeek jumped through the hole in a desperate attempt to save himself. The problem was that once fate makes up its mind, there is no going back.

A piece of debris fell on his back making him fall down. He was pinned by some heavy planks and couldn't get them off. Everything was falling and burning up around him. It was as if the fire was circling around him like he was the sun and it was the planets. As the fire slowly crept closer, he saw all of his fondest memories—his first A, his overnight school trips, his first steps, everything. All of these thoughts made him feel warm inside (and outside). He wanted to hold on to these memories forever. He felt so happy that he remembered all of these things. He wanted to go out in peace and happiness. The average kid, going out in a very unaverage way.

The next morning everybody was buzzing about their earthquake stories. Somebody was taking a walk when it happened and somebody was in the lavatory. Everybody had their own outlook on what happened that day, but there was one family who had an incredible story. A young woman talked about a strange boy who saved her and her five-month-old son Zeek Edmonds II.

Luna
Nile Randolph

For fifteen years, Luna dreaded this day. Even as a toddler, she knew something wasn't quite right. Whenever her birthday came around, adults in the house never seemed happy enough to celebrate. When she was ten, Luna learned why.

Luna's mother was half witch, but didn't want to acknowledge that part of her heritage. She did not go to schools witches ran so their children could learn spells. She also suppressed her Moon Sorcery, the supposed gift all witches inherit. Her mother married a human man, who loved her despite her half witch ancestry.

On the day Luna was born, a witch cursed her, saying that every year on her birthday, a solar eclipse would occur in her town, until she was sixteen. However, by the time Luna was sixteen, she would have completed her transformation from human to witch. It was to be punishment for her mother, to slowly watch her baby become someone she'd avoided becoming herself.

Nobody knew if the curse was true, but no one wanted to find out. So, every year on June twenty-ninth, Luna's parents kept her inside the house, afraid her slow transformation would be visible. Luna could hear her mother sobbing by the river every day for several hours, and she'd sing a song.

Born into a destiny
No one can refuse
Run away at a young age
You'll have nothing to lose

A child, a child, still sleeps in there
Cursed and one day soon
My child, my child, too proud to scare

Every year on her birthday, her mother would sing the song and splash water on her face from the river, which was said to have magical qualities. Even though Luna's mother didn't know if the magic river could have adverse consequences, she was willing to take risks.

That afternoon, Luna sat in her bedroom and looked out through the tiny window. It was the day before her sixteenth birthday, and her parents insisted that she stay inside the house, fearful of how villagers would treat her. The witches made sure everyone in town knew about her curse. Townspeople teased her and threw rocks at her when she was a child, and it could only get worse now that the curse was a day away from bearing fruit. Luna had no friends, and her parents were too scared to have more children after their firstborn had been cursed by a witch.

She felt loneliness in the pit of her stomach, but she was used to it by now. In her short sixteen years of life, she'd learned the pain isolation caused and refused to be bothered by it.

Luna could see a crowd of young boys gathering outside her window, but she couldn't tell what they were doing. She pressed her face up against the glass to get a better view when a stone came flying at her. Glass shattered in her face as the rock made direct contact with her skin, smashing her glasses and almost breaking her nose.

Luna hurried away from the shattered pane to the mirror in her bathroom. The right side of her face was covered in blood and glass. She wanted to cry, but knew she had to stay strong. Instead, Luna cleaned off her face with her house's most delicate washcloth.

As she was turning off the lights in her bathroom, Luna noticed a golden light flickering near her shower. Mesmerized, she followed the glow into the bathroom again but couldn't see it once she stepped inside. Luna rushed over to the window and saw the light once again. It floated outside, and since Luna's bathroom was on the ground floor of the house, she followed it.

Once she was out in the sun, Luna looked around to make sure her parents couldn't see her. She remembered her parents said that they were going to the market in the town square, so she dashed across the long field of soft dandelions into the woods. Tall trees provided a little too much shade, and there was a slight wind. Luna hugged herself so that she could warm up.

The light appeared again, close enough so that Luna could see what it really was. It had a body like a human's, but it also had wings. A fairy had been guiding her.

"Luna, follow me to your true destiny," the fairy said.

"Why do you guide me? I am a witch," Luna said.

"You are not a witch. This quest will help free you from any witch's bond, including your curse." The fairy smiled proudly at her. "But we must be quick. You must complete the quest before sunrise tomorrow, or you will become a witch."

Luna continued walking beside the glowing ·fairy, who hovered near her shoulder. She didn't understand why the fairy was worried. It was barely afternoon.

They stopped at a desolate place in the forest where all the trees were bare. Crows flew from branch to branch, catching whatever they could find to eat, even their own species.

"The quest has three parts. Witches have a saying: 'Face your fears and slay your demons.' We are now at the Forest of Sorrows, where you will face your three greatest nightmares," the fairy announced. "If you cry, scream, or do anything out of emotion during these Fear Presentations, you will be disqualified from the quest. I will not be there to help you. Go on now."

Luna walked into the forest, and it became eerily colder as she reached its depths. She shuddered at the sound of a crow's call. This part of the forest was completely dark, and Luna felt very alone. Unsure of the consequences, she took one last step.

Suddenly, a group of crows began to circle her. There were twenty-nine of them. She couldn't see them, but she could feel them, each connected to the other. The crows called out to her, a shrill sound she couldn't ignore. She covered her ears with her hands, but it was not enough.

Slowly, the Forest of Sorrows melted away, and Luna was presented with her first fear.

In her first vision, it smelled like bread in her house as Luna's mother wrapped Luna in a blanket. The baby smiled and giggled, giddy from her mother's touch. Then, the witch came to curse Luna. Instead of protecting her, her mother took her out by the river and floated her away in a basket.

Luna's head ached from the vision, but she steadied herself for the second fear.

Luna saw herself in the town square alone. She looked to be about ten years old. She was walking with a basket of cookies when a man ran up to her and pushed her to the ground. Then he kicked her repeatedly in her side as the rest of the people in the town square joined in. Young Luna curled up into a ball as villagers assaulted her with words and blows, leaving her with many scars on her body and in her heart.

Luna had a terrible urge to cry, but she pinched her right palm, causing physical pain to take away emotional pain.

The last vision was of Luna's near future. She was standing on a steep cliff, and there were witches all around her. The witches were inducting her into their coven, and the trial was to jump off the cliff and use her gifts to land. Since Luna was assumed to have the Moon Sorcery, she jumped off and said a quick spell. However, Luna's gifts were too weak, and she landed on the ground at the bottom of the cliff, her body limp.

Luna's eyes burned and her chin quivered, and she knew this was her fate. She breathed deeply, but couldn't deny the years of pain and isolation that had caused her to hide her emotions. Luna swallowed, doing her best to bury her feelings deep inside her throat.

It worked.

Luna was transported back to the forest where the fairy was waiting. She was tired and out of breath.

"I slayed the demons for you," the fairy said, smiling sadly. "The witches will come after me. Listen: you must go to the river and sing your mother's song."

"But I don't know the whole thing!" Luna bawled.

"You will know, you will . . ." Just as the fairy was about to finish, the large, gnarled, filthy hands of the oldest witch sent a sharp, black arrow through the fairy's tiny body. As the fairy fell to the ground, her golden light slowly dimmed.

Luna knew she had to get to the river before sunrise, so she ran, the witch who killed the Fairy close on her heels. Her feet barely touched the ground as she felt the cool night's winds peaceful embrace. Her curly raven hair bounced in its ponytail as Luna skidded to a stop.

She kneeled at the river, splashed water on her face, and sang:

Born into a destiny
No one can refuse
Run away at a young age
You'll have nothing to lose

A child, a child, still sleeps in there
Cursed and one day soon
My child, my child, too proud to scare
Will see the sun, not moon

Through Their Lenses

Lived for validation
A human could not bring
Born beside a river
Where mothers often sing

A child, a child, still sleeps in there
Cursed by wicked ways
My child, my child, sleep tight, my dear
You'll see the light of day.

A glowing silver light circled Luna as she stood up. The witch raised her bow, but Luna's feet could not run. They were planted in the ground like the trees of the forest.

Suddenly, the light disappeared. A black moon tattoo appeared on Luna's wrist. The sun began to rise. The hole in her heart was filled, and she knew the curse was broken.

Gone Girls Float

Kira Chen

Mama didn't like me saying she was dead, so instead we always said Bee was *missing*. Missing for five years after they found her footsteps leading to the lake and then ending, missing after they spent days diving into the waters to try to retrieve her, missing after they couldn't even find the gold bracelet she was wearing that day or the white dress she'd put on in the morning. Sometimes, when I go down to that lake, I imagine the dress, floating ghostlike through the depths.

I wonder if I'll find it—or her—some days, but then other days I don't think about it at all and instead I just slip through the surface and into the lake. The waters are always freezing, and when you dip under them, it feels like your bones are turning to ice and your skin to frost. One of these days, Mama will come down to find me and I'll just be a solid block of ice slowly melting into the lake.

After all, Bee went missing and Dad left so it's only natural that eventually I should go missing too. The kids already whisper about our family being cursed, and it costs nothing to prove them right.

We've always been the outliers. The strangers in a ferociously close-knit circle. I push away from the bank and slip underwater. It's warmer in the summer, thin shafts of sunlight warming the water slightly. Well, slightly warmer, at least, like a light dusting of snow against my skin instead of the chill that bites through skin to bone.

The lake is something of a legend in the town, or rather, a source of almost all the legends in the town. No one knows how deep it goes, but stories abound of people who tried to find out. None of them made it out, supposedly. Or maybe some of them did, and the generations of tales have twisted it all around. Maybe in years, the details of what happened to Bee will be forgotten too, replaced with made-up whispers and jokes.

Perhaps the whispers and jokes are already here.

Swimming in the lake my sister probably drowned in five years ago is an interesting experience. Everyone worries about me when I tell them about this hobby of mine, and I don't know how to tell them that underwater, I can finally find a place away from the constant noise of murmurs and giggles and stares.

Underwater, everything is clear. And everything is silent. And there are only two directions that really matter: up and down. Under the surface and above. I stay under the surface as long as possible, holding my breath until my lungs feel like they're going to explode.

I gasp, breaking the surface, and in the open air, I'm smiling.

That's when I realize I've been wearing my sneakers the whole time; I frown at my feet, swim to the bank, and haul myself up onto the rocks. After retying my shoes, I push my hair away from my face and slip back into the water. Because what else is there to do—go home?

It's dark and cold all around me—the water gets murky at the surface, and I've learned that if I want to be able to see anything, I've got to swim deeper, farther down. Down here, I can't feel anything, and when I open my eyes, I can see through the water for yards.

Not for the first time, I turn my gaze toward the bottom of the lake, the one so far away I can't see it. It's lost in a cloud of...dust or whatever that is.

I'm paddling down, movements slowed by the push and pull of the current, and something soft brushes against my finger. White fabric floating through the water. And in the middle, a dot of red—*red-stitched flowers*. Bee disappeared wearing her white dress, the one stitched with red flowers.

No, that isn't possible—she's gone—the dress disappeared. But here it is, clear as day, and all I can think is that I have to follow it. I reach out instinctively, but it dances away from my grip, floating deeper underwater.

Keep swimming, keep swimming. Part of me knows it's most likely not Bee's dress, but the other part of me, the hopeful, wishing part of me, keeps me moving. Keep swimming. Hands pushing through the water, deeper, deeper, deeper. The dress is just out of my reach, every single time.

I push forward once more, propelling myself through the water, snatching at the dress as quickly as I can. My hand closes around it, and I almost cheer—*even if it's not really hers, even if it can't be hers.*

My lungs burn. I start to swim up, but it's too dark. I'm too far down. Where is the surface and where is the bottom of the lake?

No, no, no, no, no. I won't drown today. I push up through the water, whichever way I think is up. It's too far. I'm too far gone. Maybe this is what it was always leading to, all these years of swimming. Maybe it was just a way to stall time before the lake took me too.

Something grabs my arm—someone. Suddenly, we're flying up through the water, too fast. Before I have time to turn and look at whoever's holding me, we're breaking the surface.

I gasp and paddle to the shore, the weight melting away from my arm. There, I lay the dress out and climb to my feet.

White fabric, that scratchy type. Red flowers, each made of delicate threads woven together.

This is her clothing.

But it can't be.

Someone laughs behind me, a light sound. I almost jump out of my skin.

"You found my dress!" a girl laughs.

Years and years of exhaustion over Mama not letting herself believe Bee was dead, and yet, when I turn and see my sister standing behind me, somehow I'm not surprised at all.

"But," I hear myself say, a note of wonder in my voice, "you're gone."

"No, I'm not."

Bee crouches down on the rocks, wrapping her arms around her knees.

Her wide eyes are distant, staring into the water. "I'm here, Angie. I just left for a little bit."

I watch her for a moment. It's in that moment that I know I was lying to myself every single time I whispered that Bee was dead.

Because a piece of me always knew she wasn't.

"Then where did you go?" I'm sitting down, hands braced against the rocks. They're covered with moss and slippery, and if I shift my foot to the wrong patch, I'll slide down into the water.

Bee leans back. "Well, I wanted to leave. And so I pretended to."

I reach out to her. I want to hug her, to know that she's real.

My hand touches her shoulder, and she grabs my wrist. Her eyes are wide with sudden fear and anger.

"Angie," she gasps, "I want to stay."

"You can stay!" I stand, trying to yank my wrist out of her grasp.

"No! I can't!" Bee's panicked, and in her panic, she stumbles forward and I stumble back. My foot hits a patch of moss. I fall backward into the water. My hand snatches out to grab Bee, but I can't touch her.

She's shimmering, and then she's gone again.

I'm in the water, cold all around me, and Bee is gone. And when I slip farther and farther down until I can't tell which way is up, I don't try anymore.

Maybe today, I'll find the bottom of the lake.

Lucky Encounter
Tara Callinan

Once upon a time, in the 1700s, there lived a wizard called Rell. He was the most infamous wizard of the century. The reason for his unpopularity was that he had been born into one of the highest wizarding family of his time and yet he had inherited absolutely no wizarding talent at all. He could barely perform the easiest of spells. When Rell finished school, he graduated on one condition: that he become a lower wizard. That was a big shame to Rell's fine family name. His parents banished him from the family home in their disappointment. Rell was officially an underdog. But most readers are probably wondering why poor unfortunate Rell was so ridiculously bad at wizardry. To those who are wondering, I will hope to give you a satisfactory answer. Wizardry is a particularly strong and powerful source of magic, and so, it must be handled carefully and in responsible hands. The art of wizardry also involves determination and fierceness, plus a good bit of shouting to keep it from setting your hair on fire. It is a lot like training a lion cub. It will quite willingly try to bite your arm off. Rell just wasn't that type of person. His characteristics were quite useless tools when it came to wizardry. Rell was very shy and hated to be bossy. His voice was hard to hear and annoyingly squeaky. It reminded you of a tiny, scared, and harmless mouse. Rell was also a bit of a chicken. He was as unferocious as it gets. It should be very clear to you by now why Rell failed at wizardry.

The next few years of Rell's life were spent being a complete loser and weren't very interesting. For the sake of the reader's patience, I will skip a few years ahead. By the time Rell was thirty-five, times were hard for wizards. More and more wizards were being eaten by the Dark Magic Disease, an uncommon virus that went around every hundred years or so. Adults rarely caught the virus, but wizard children were in high risk of catching it. The practice of wizardry had a chance of dying out, for the children were the only future. This was tragic news for wizards, so to prevent the end of wizardry, the highest wizards (wizards who ran the government) had taken to high precautions. Every wizard must marry the daughter of a wizard and the couple were to have children. If the wizard failed to have children, he would be thrown out of the entire wizarding society and would be jinxed so that he couldn't perform wizardry. Rell couldn't count how many times he had got down on one knee and proposed—from the prettiest to the ugliest of women, from the wittiest and most charming to the unmannerly and dim-witted, from the sensible and practical to the utterly featherheaded, from the most honorable families to the ones with the most average family trees. All of them refused. They knew very well that Rell was the most undesirable person to marry. Rell was 99.999 percent sure that he was going to be kicked out of the world of wizardry any day now. The 0.001 percent glimmer of hope had long been forgotten. It didn't matter anymore. He was absolutely miserable.

***

One day, Rell was having a walk in the woods for his own pleasure. He came to a clearing in the woods where there was a magnificent manor. Just then, Rell noticed a girl that was staggering and was being kicked and scolded by a person with a cruel female voice. The girl had bruises all over her leg and looked much too thin. She stumbled toward Rell, teardrops falling onto her ripped black dress. Her ragged auburn hair was coming loose from her bun and her big round eyes were red.

"Well, you look in a right state. What's the matter?" Rell said as kindly and softly as he could.

"I b-broke the b-best plates, and I'm b-banished from the house for a week," stammered the girl tearfully. She let out a high-pitched sob.

"Oh dear. I do that all the time. They made a big deal out of it, didn't they?"

"Yes," the girl said resentfully.

"Well, don't worry. I'll help you," Rell said consolingly. "I'm going to take you in to my cottage for a week. It will be a bit cramped with two people, but it won't be that bad."

"But why are you helping me? I'm not a charity case, you know," said the girl.

"I'm helping you because where I come from, I'm infamous. You'll keep me company," Rell said earnestly.

She looks half starved! Rell thought.

"Okay, I suppose I've nowhere else to go," the girl said hesitantly. "I forgot to ask you—what's your name?"

"Rell."

"Yours?"

"Marianne."

***

"We're nearly there," Rell announced.

They landed in a dodgy part of town. There was just enough light to see a couple of cracked and broken windows. The cottages were in need of a fresh coat of paint. There was a faint smell of tobacco in the air.

Marianne shivered. *This place is freaky*, she thought.

Rell could see the unhidden dislike fixed on Marianne's face. "I know it's a bit eerie," he said. "But it's all I have."

Marianne looked guilty. "Sorry," she mumbled.

"It's fine," Rell said kindly. "Now, my house is number thirteen."

It was next to a seemingly deserted cottage with broken windows and no door. Rell stepped inside and lit a candle. There was a small, cramped room painted an ugly peach.

"This is the living room, where you'll be sleeping," he said.

At the side of the room was a faded pink armchair and a lengthy bookshelf. On the other side of the room was a window with black curtains.

"Do you want something to eat?" Rell asked.

Marianne nodded.

"The third door is the way to the backyard, which has two big buckets for your call of nature," Rell said.

After they ate, they both went to bed. Despite its ugliness and its shabby whereabouts, Marianne liked the cottage.

At least Rell doesn't slap or hit me. And I expected him to be bossier. Maybe he even likes me, Marianne thought drowsily as she curled up into a ball and fell asleep.

***

Marianne woke up. She had been here for two days now. She had really gotten to know Rell, and he knew a lot about her too. Rell told Marianne his life story and poured out all his sorrows. Rell had let down his famous family by becoming a lower wizard. He was banished from his family home, which Marianne thought was quite cruel. He had lived in the cottage for fifteen years. He didn't exactly enjoy life, but dreams of becoming a mediocre wizard had kept him going. Marianne told Rell about how her parents had died in a carriage accident, and because she had no known living relatives, she was forced to accept a job as a maid in return for food and a bed. She had been a maid since she was nine.

She opened her eyes, brushed off the sand in them, stretched, and walked out of the sitting room. As she entered the kitchen, Marianne met a bleary-eyed Rell.

"Good morning," he said. "Breakfast is on the table. Already had mine. Same old buttered bread."

"You made breakfast?" asked Marianne. She had made breakfast so far.

"I did. I figured it's my turn to get up a bit earlier," said Rell.

Clang, clang!

Rell went to get the door. When he came back, he was reading the front page of the newspaper with concern and panic.

"What's the matter?" Marianne questioned.

"The guards will start patrolling the houses looking for single wizards at exactly half past six. That's in forty-five minutes!" he murmured worriedly. "Oh dear, oh dear!"

"Okay, we are in a bad situation here, but if we calm down and think, we might come up with a temporary solution," said Marianne.

"But how are we going to find a woman who will pretend to be my wife in only forty-five minutes!?" Rell fretted.

"Um, well, maybe I could pretend to be your wife," suggested Marianne.

"Listen, I'll make a deal with you. If you pretend to be my wife for the wizard guards, you can stay here as long as you want, no catch, and you can have a bit of food for breakfast and dinner," squeaked Rell.

Marianne couldn't help feeling sorry for him. "Well, I've made up my mind. I'll agree to the deal if you teach me some wizarding tricks."

"Deal!" said Rell.

***

The police walked menacingly to the door. They looked quite powerful and scary.

"So, Rell, you managed to get a wife who was poor enough to respect you,'"one of the guards sneered.

"As a matter of fact, I did," Rell retorted.

Marianne glared at the guards.

"I bet she couldn't even bring in a bad dowry, she's so poor," another guard taunted.

"You seem very young to be marrying a thirty-year-old," the guard said.

"Girls much younger than me marry," said Marianne defiantly. "And they marry older men."

"Whatever," said the guard. "Come on, guys, let's get out of here. We're just wasting our time. There are so many more houses to go to."

As soon as Rell closed the front door, his shoulders sagged and he sighed in relief. Marianne relaxed too and she laughed in relief.

"Thank god that's over," she said.

At that moment the same thought crossed their minds: *This could be fun after all!*

Not Too Late

Mara Bech

Marjorie cannot sleep tonight. Her bones creak as she slowly gets out of bed and shuffles to the kitchen. It's really the kitchenette, for the small apartments in the retirement community are equipped only with a two-burner stove, toaster oven, and small refrigerator. It's been an adjustment for her, but then, all her life has been spent adjusting to new circumstances. The large digital clock glows green. 12:47.

Marjorie flicks on the light, then looks through the cupboards in search of some cocoa. Hopefully that will help her relax. As she sets the kettle on to boil, Marjorie looks around the small living room and kitchen. She looks at the skin on her hands, practically translucent. She can see every vein and bone. Her fingers ache from arthritis and her back hunches over with the weight of her worries. She is exhausted every day and sometimes wonders why she is still alive. The doctor added an antidepressant to her boatload of medications when she mentioned it at her last appointment.

The kettle is whistling now, and the aroma of chocolate fills the air. Marjorie ambles over to the sofa and sets her mug down. She takes her photo albums from the shelf and settles into the velvety cushions under a homemade afghan, knitted out of purple wool—her favorite color.

Marjorie turns the pages, the nostalgic scent of paste wafting up from the yellowed books. Here she is, 1941, a little girl, grinning as she holds a kitten. A photograph of her first-grade class, with the words in her mother's handwriting. *My baby. So grown up.* Marjorie remembers how excited she was to put together photograph albums for her own children. There are a few newspaper clippings, too, mostly about the war. She puts the 1940 album back and selects 1963. Here are all of her wedding photos. Her wrinkled, slightly pinched face softens into a smile as she reminisces about her veil, the beautiful lilacs she carried, her father's proud face as he gave her away. She remembers the light, airy dresses her bridesmaids wore, with purple sashes to match the flowers, and recalls chuckling with Carl afterward about the congested minister. Marjorie grows somber as she turns the pages, seeing her handwriting, shaky beneath a picture of Carl in uniform. He was never the same once he came back from Vietnam. His eyes, which had been so full of life before, were gray with fear when he returned; in the middle of the night he would wake, sweating, shaking, out of his mind with terror. The trauma in his brain, the doctor said, led to the stroke that killed him. Marjorie looks at the wall. Carl was at peace now, or at least that is what she liked to think. She does not remember the last time she felt at peace. It seemed as if she had always been given burdens to carry. *Yes,* Marjorie thinks. *Even when I was young I had burdens to carry.* She smiles again when she turns to a blurry photograph of baby Roger, arms waving, feet in the air. The next album is filled with photos of Roger's birthday parties and his school pictures. Now Roger is married and has children. *My, how time does fly.*

Marjorie shuffles over to the mantel and takes down Roger's Christmas card. She has only seen her grandchildren once, on account of the fact that they live on the other side of the country. She misses them. They probably don't remember her, though. She tucks the card with the smiling family on it into Roger's album, next to the greeting cards that were sent at Easter and Halloween and served as a reminder to the son she never saw anymore.

Moving on to the next album, Marjorie feels a slight ache in her stomach. Maybe the hot cocoa did not agree with her. The cream-colored leather album has the name *Valerie* embossed on it in shiny pink. Her breath catches in her throat, but she forces herself to open the album. A smiling baby girl. A round toddler proudly holding a doll. Photos from first, second, third grade. Marjorie has tears running down her face. The heat of anger mixed with the saltiness of sorrow runs down her face. *My baby.* A caption under a picture of Valerie smiling up at the world, innocent, happy. *So grown up.* How did Valerie go from smiling, happy, to the woman whose voice had been so full of hate and fury the last time Marjorie talked to her? Valerie's voice. Marjorie hasn't heard her daughter's voice in years. Fourteen years, to be precise, but the relationship between the two had been rocky long before then. Another stab of pain—that cocoa did not agree with her stomach at all, Marjorie thinks—brings her back into the present. She is bitter. Valerie never called back after that day. She never called to apologize. The throbbing in her stomach has moved to her chest, and Marjorie feels nauseous. She lies down on the couch, but she finds herself getting up and walking to the counter. She picks up the phone from its cradle. She dials Roger's number. The clock beams a bright 3:28. The call goes to voicemail and Marjorie speaks. "Roger, I'm just calling to say hello. I'm feeling a bit restless tonight, but I wanted you to know that I love you and your family. I miss you, too. Maybe you can visit this year. Good night, my Roger-bear," she says, using her nickname for him when he was small. "I love you." She hangs up just as agonizing pain rips through her chest. Marjorie sinks onto a chair with the phone in her hand. She is dizzy, but she needs to do this now. Marjorie takes a deep breath and calls Valerie.

The call goes to voicemail, as Marjorie expected. It will be easier this way. They can talk together later. "Valerie. It's Marjorie." Valerie had stopped calling her Mom a long time ago. "I'm calling to say…that I'm sorry for breaking our relationship and not trying to put it back together. I said so many things that night that I regret. But what I regret most of all is that I never tried to talk to you again. I was a bad mother. I don't know where you are now, but I never should have let my anger and sorrow create a wall between us. Please call me, Valerie. You can scream or swear at me, but just call. I need to hear your voice and I need to mend my fences before it's too late. I love you, Valerie. Please forgive me."

Marjorie's voice breaks. She ends the call and cries for a while. The pain intensifies, and Marjorie, hunched over in agony, makes it to her room holding on to the wall. She sinks into her bed, and, finally, feeling as if a burden has been lifted from her shoulders, slips into peaceful rest.

✢✢✢

She wasn't going to the funeral. That life was behind her now. And besides, she was far too busy to fly across the country just for a church service. People would talk, but, let them talk. She wouldn't be there to hear it. It's been a long day, and Valerie sits down on the couch to listen to her voicemail. There's a number she hasn't seen in a while. She is bitter about this call—it means her mother got the last word, because she was dead now. Still, something makes her listen. Valerie gasps as the message begins to play. She stuffs some clothes into a suitcase and drives to the airport, her mind racing. She catches a late flight and plays the message again and again until her phone dies. It's a long flight, and Valerie tries to sleep, but her mother's voice is resonating in her head. *Before it's too late.* She was too late. Her mother had called her on the night she died. The sun rises as the plane touches down on the tarmac. Valerie drives to the church, where her brother is talking with some people in the foyer. She slips unnoticed into the chapel. Her mother's coffin is surrounded by purple lilacs. She touches Marjorie's cold hand. "I'm sorry. I was too late." Her breath ragged, with tears streaming down her face, Valerie says the words that would have been so hard to say only a week ago. "I love you, Mom."

The Attack of King Covid

Arjun Bajwa

King Covid looks over his kingdom and remembers that today is the day that he takes over the world. King Covid is a chubby, short man with brown eyes and black hair. He is very greedy and usually a rude person. "All generals gather in the strategy room!" he shouts.

"Thank you all for being here. Today is going to be a really big day for us," he roars. "We now have to plan the attack."

After a few moments, General 1 speaks up. "I think we should send soldiers to every continent."

"I don't know if that would be the best idea," King Covid says.

Next comes General 2 and 4's idea. "General 4 and I think that we should start with Russia because it is the biggest country in the world."

"Yes, but it's just the biggest country, but it doesn't really have a lot of people. We need to attack something that will impact a lot of people."

General 3 speaks up "How about we go for the country with the most population, China. China has the most population in the world so it will leave the whole world alarmed."

"Yes, now that is a great idea!" King Covid exclaims.

"After we take over China, we can continue to spread through the rest of Asia," General 4 says.

"Inform the soldiers," King Covid orders firmly.

After telling all the soldiers about the plan, they start to carry it out. They send the soldiers to China, and then they start checking the news for any updates.

After a few days, they see on the news that the first case of the coronavirus has been confirmed.

"Yes, finally the first case!" King Covid says. "It's about time we get some good news," he says.

Everyone cheers.

Every day King Covid monitors the news to see if there have been any developments, and one day when he's watching, he see something. "NO!" he shouts.

King Covid gathers up all the generals again.

"Hello, everyone, the reason I have gathered you all here today is because the humans have found out that wearing a mask reduces the chances of them getting the virus. This is going to be really bad for us!" King Covid utters. "Let's just hope that the humans don't wear masks. It is highly likely because it isn't very comfortable..." King Covid trails off.

One month later, King Covid decides that it is time to start spreading the virus throughout the rest of the world.

A few weeks later, King Covid is watching the news and he sees that they are starting to do worldwide lockdowns. "NO this isn't good! If they start lockdowns, then no one will interact and spread the virus. Those stupid humans. This is going to delay our mission by a lot!" King Covid raged.

After a few weeks of the virus spreading all over the world, King Covid checks the news. "Now that the virus has gone mostly everywhere in the world let's check the news and see how the humans are handling this pandemic," King Covid says deviously. "All generals report to the strategy room now!"

Once all the generals arrive, King Covid turns on the TV and everyone sees that most people aren't wearing masks. King Covid and all the generals start laughing.

"Wow, they aren't even wearing masks!" King Covid laughed. "It's like they're asking to get the coronavirus!"

General 3 chuckled. "These humans are dumber than I thought."

General 2 cackles.

"SHUT UP, EVERYONE," King Covid barks. "When those humans get sick, they are going to regret not wearing a mask. Now we wait and let the soldiers do their job."

One day, General 3 is watching the news and he thinks, *Why are we doing this to the humans? I know some humans are bad and all, but not everyone is bad. Not everyone deserves to lose their loved ones. Most people are innocent and good. Why should they have to suffer if they're innocent? Why are we destroying this beautiful Earth?*

"Oh no, I need to go tell King Covid right away!" General 3 says.

"King Covid, we can't do this. We have to call back the soldiers now before things get out of hand!" he says.

"No! Who do you think you are that you can just walk in here and tell me what to do!" King Covid says.

"But, sir, innocent people are dying!" General 3 says.

"I don't care! They deserve it after what they did to us!" King Covid shouts.

"Yes, but we must forget the past and move on. We can't keep on clinging to something that happened so long ago. If we don't, more people will lose their lives, and that unfair! The innocent humans do not deserve to be punished!" General 3 says.

"Say one more word and watch what will happen to you!" King Covid screams.

Then General 3 walks away frightened.

"King Covid can't do this! I don't care what he says. I am going to call the soldiers back!" General 3 says. Then General 3 goes to the telephone. "Hello, soldiers, we all saw how the mission is going, so good job for that, but King Covid has given me orders to call the mission off, so please make your way back to Planet Covid."

"Yes, sir, we will be there shortly," Lieutenant 1 replies.

"Okay, good."

"One thing I want to say, sir, is that Earth is so magnificent. The sun is always glistening, and the clouds look so fluffy and silky. The freshly cut grass is so pleasant, and the air is so clean, and the whole purity of the Earth, in general, is just so spectacular."

"Yes, I completely agree with you, lieutenant. I, too, wish I could be there to experience the astonishing Earth."

"GENERAL 3, WHAT ARE YOU DOING?" King Covid interrupted.

"Sir, I am so sorry, but it had to be done."

"Wow, you are really confident, but now you are going to have to pay the price. You know I can't believe that I ever trusted you!"

Now I know you all are thinking, *Why does King Covid hate the humans so much?* Well, let me tell you a story. Many years ago, King Covid was very good friends with King Earth. King Earth always visited each other's kingdoms, but one day King Covid and King Earth were sitting eating lunch, but King Earth had put something in King Covid's food. After King Covid ate the food, he got really sick, and when King Covid found out, he got really mad. After that, King Covid stopped talking to King Earth, and he also stopped going to his kingdom. That is why King Covid wants to spread coronavirus through all of Earth to get revenge on King Earth for doing that to him.

"King Covid, I am really sorry, but you need to forgive him. You can't hold a grudge for something that happened so many years ago. Also, he only meant it as a joke. He never meant for you to get that sick. Please just forgive him!"

"You're right, I really miss him, and he's my best friend. I will call him right now, and I will tell him that I forgive him."

"Yes, sir, that is the spirit. Now you should call him."

Then King Covid calls King Earth. "Hi, Earth, I just wanted to call you and let you know that I forgive you for what you did, and I am also really sorry. Can you please forgive me!"

"Hi, Covid, of course I forgive you. You are my best friend and I will never forget that."

"I have already called my soldiers back so they will no longer spread the virus, and once again I am really sorry."

"Thank you for doing this, Earth."

"Thank you, General 3, for telling me to do this. I would never have made up with Earth if it wasn't for you, so thank you!"

"No problem, sir. I am always there for you."

Molten Souls

Elijah Bodden

Absina slipped through the crack that separated her from the ravine outside and deftly climbed up the blazing rock wall, ignoring the shouts of her family to return to their cave. Although she knew how much trouble she would be in when she got home, she had to know what her parents were keeping her from. Absina took in a deep breath as she reached the top of the ravine, marveling at the beauty of the planet. Marveling at lakes of molten lava, much like the one in her cave but far larger, at vast mountains of pure black rock, at cracks that shattered the perfect smoothness of the planet, somehow making it even more beautiful. Through these cracks, the molten interior of the planet exposed itself, in much the same way her body—and those of all Molten Souls—gave way to the fiery core just underneath the surface.

She could not believe she had lived her entire life in her cave, never knowing the sheer beauty that lay just outside its entrance. How had her parents kept her from this? All because they were afraid of these supposed "surface dwellers."

Suddenly, a thunderous roar ripped her from her thoughts. She spun around to find a mountain of a creature towering over her. It looked like Absina in its cracked, rocky skin and molten interior, but that's where the similarities ended. Where Absina had small, clawless feet, it had massive talons, its legs were thicker than Absina's entire body, and instead of a harmless, toothless mouth as Absina had, it had a muscular snout, with daggerlike teeth.

Run, she told her legs, but they were rooted to the spot. All she could think of was the stories of what the surface dwellers had done to cave dwellers like herself in the past.

Two more Molten Souls, one built much like the first, only bulkier, and the other sleek and streamlined, but both as massive as the first, strode up to stand on either side of it.

"What's going on?" grunted the biggest one.

"What does it look like to you, Thur?" The first flicked a cinder at Absina. "This little runt—what is he anyway, a rat?—was just sitting there, on *my* ledge, as if he owned it, so now I'm going to teach him a lesson."

"But it's so small and helpless looking, and I bet it didn't even know that was your ledge," said the smallest of the three.

"Just shut up, both of you idiots!" snapped the first Molten Soul.

He took a careful step forward, a hungry look in his eyes as he prepared to lunge. Absina squeezed her eyes shut, bracing herself for whatever was about to happen.

What felt like an eternity later, Absina saw a flash of light through her squeezed eyelids. She felt something like a release of tension inside her, as if a door that had been shut in her head had suddenly been blown open. For a moment, Absina thought she was dead. But that couldn't be, since she could still feel the warm ground beneath her feet. And anyway, would she even be able to think if she were dead?

Finally, her curiosity got the better of her, and she opened one eye a fraction, unsure what she would see.

She scrambled back, shocked by the view in front of her. Right there, where the surface dwellers had been just moments ago, stood a massive wall of volcanic rock. She stepped closer to peer through a hole in the rock and spotted all three surface dwellers running at top speed away from her.

In the very back of her head, a thought arose: *Did I do that?*

When she searched it out, Absina was still able to feel that same openness as if that door in her mind was still open. Absina explored this new feeling. It felt as if she was truly connected to the planet, as if the rock, the magma, the clouds, the entire planet was calling out to her.

The urge was too strong to resist.

She stepped forward to a small stream of lava and stretched out her arm, testing. As she came closer to the lava, she noticed a slight resistance, as if the air was thicker closer to the surface than anywhere else. Absina pushed harder, drawing her arm closer and closer to the surface. She felt a sudden release of tension, and the lava began to move, a small depression forming in the surface. The nearer she drew her hand to it, the farther the lava withdrew from her reach. Suddenly, she pulled her hand from the surface, and the lava followed, forming a bubble on the surface. She pulled farther, and a small orb of magma disconnected from the rest and rose into the air. When she looked closer, Absina discovered that it wasn't just the lava, but several small stones that were following her actions in midair. Finally, Absina released the feeling in her mind, and just as she had somehow expected, the lava, along with the stones, splashed back down into the stream of magma.

***

Absina let the pile of boulders collapse back to the ground next to the lava lake with a crash, exhausted but relieved that the day's training was over. Ever since she had first discovered her ability to manipulate magma and stone, she had been training relentlessly, pushing her limits and becoming better at controlling it. One day she would claim her revenge on the other Molten Souls for all they had done to the cave dwellers. For making them feel weak and defenseless, for taking advantage of them, and for driving them underground in the first place. She would bring her family back to the surface. And they would never need to fear the surface dwellers again.

She was certainly growing stronger, becoming able to control larger and larger objects, and pretty soon, she would carry out her plan.

Although it would have been easier to tell her parents, she had kept her ability a secret. She would surprise them at the last moment, bringing them to the surface with her.

Absina decided to try one last thing before she finished training for the day. She braced herself, searched out the feeling, and then strained to move the entire lava lake at once.

The lava hardly moved.

She forced it as hard as she could, and finally, she began to see the lava shift a bit. With the little energy she had left, she gave one last push. The feeling in the back of her head became suddenly painful, and she was knocked off her feet by a violent crash.

Something was horribly wrong.

Struggling to her feet, she rushed to the crack in the wall and peered out into the ravine. It was a horrible sight. The walls of the ravine had shattered open and cracked apart, and lava was pouring in rapidly.

This had to be her fault.

She needed to warn her family. But just then, she heard a desperate call for help, coming from somewhere on the surface outside the ravine. Although she hated every one of the surface dwellers, Absina couldn't just let someone die. She climbed deftly up the treacherous sides of the ravine, yelling at the top of her lungs to her family to get out.

Absina reached the top ledge of the ravine, fighting her way over the fractured surface. It looked as if the old surface had been shattered, with gaping cracks spanning the length of the planet, almost as if it was tearing itself apart.

She leaped over the edge of the ravine and immediately saw who had called for help. A young-looking Molten Soul stood directly in the path of the lava flooding up from one of the new cracks.

Absina hesitated for one instant as she considered letting the lava overtake the child.

However, she sprang into action seconds later, horrified at herself for even thinking of letting anyone die.

Absina reached the Molten Soul just in time. She arced the lava upward and over herself and the child, and it cooled into a stone arch above them.

Absina jumped as she heard another call for help rise from the plain, then another, and another. There were simply too many Molten Souls in danger; there was no way to save everyone.

There was only one thing she could try to undo the damage she had caused.

Absina took a deep breath, planted her feet, and closed her eyes. For the last time, she searched out the feeling.

Pain coursed through her mind, her body, her heart, everything that had feeling.

But her plan miraculously seemed to be working. The shattered plates of the planet slowly, almost unnoticeably, shifted back together, the lava stopped flowing, and then slowly reversed back into the cracks.

Absina gritted her teeth at the pain as the sheets of rock slowly fused into one. And, although she realized she was going to die, Absina was at peace, for she had done her best to save the planet. And it had worked.

Out of the corner of her eye, she saw her family safely standing on the ledge above their ravine, and she knew she could finally let go.

Absina released the tension, and just like the first glob of lava floating above the stream, Absina fell back to the ground.

How I Tamed a Shapeshifter
Ashritha Vuddharaju

How I tamed a shapeshifter? What? Are shapeshifters for real? What? Did I really tame a shapeshifter? What? You must be thinking I'm making up this story for a class project or something, right? No, I'm not. I'll narrate you the most exciting episode of how it all happened. But before that, you need to know a little about me.

Hey, everyone, my name is Georgia Jacklin Banks. I am a bold and beautiful ten-year-old girl from Hawaii. I always wanted a pet, but since I have a two-year-old sister and a six-year-old brother, I'm not allowed to have one. Guess why? Because my parents are terrified that my siblings might get bitten or scratched. I mean really. I do find that funny.

All right, want to hear about my thrilling adventure? Well, let's begin. On one fine, bright, and early morning, I was near a volcano, when I saw a large shadow on the ground. I looked up and saw a huge green scaly dinosaur. I immediately hid behind a nearby tree. I didn't know if this beast was a prehistoric predator. While I was hiding, I saw the dino sniff the air. I figured it could smell me, so I frantically looked around for a way to camouflage my smell. I saw a big, deep pile of mud and jumped in as quickly and silently as possible. I poked my head out and saw that the dino was looking the other way.

Once I had finally stopped panicking, I realized that this dino was the king of dinos. He was the Tyrannosaurus rex! I thanked my lucky star that my reflexes told me to hide or I would be dead meat, literally! That's when I made another shocking discovery that there was a dragon! The rest happened in a bit of a blur.

The dinosaur heard me gasp at the dragon and came charging at me. The dragon that was noticeably larger than the dino heard the T-rex charge at me. The T-rex picked me up

Award-Winning Short Stories by Tweens

and the dragon picked the T-rex up. The dragon then started to fly up and slightly to the north. It was taking us over the ocean.

The T-rex looked scared and dropped me in the ocean. While I was falling, I saw a green blob above me fall as well. Then I crashed into the water. I can swim very well since I live on an island. So I wasn't that worried. When I emerged from the water, the green blob nearly fell on my head. That's when I finally got a good look at the green blob. It was a baby T-rex!

My first instinct was to grab the poor thing and swim it to safety, but I realized that it was a dangerous beast that had been extinct for 65.5 million years. While I was debating my options, the dino turned into a baby human! Now I knew it was dangerous and risky, but I really wanted to study this specimen. So I scooped the human T-rex (Human-rex) thing into my hands and placed him on my back.

After about twenty minutes, we reached the shore. I placed the Human-rex on the beach tenderly, hoping it would shapeshift into something else, but it didn't. It just sat there looking at me like a normal baby. We sat there for another ten minutes or so, when I thought of something.

I walked away from the Human-rex. Then the Human-rex started crawling toward me. Once it got close to me, I sprinted away. The Human-rex looked sad and turned into a small, green creature. I snuck up on the creature, and it turned around. It let out a horrible scream and turned into a human again.

I sat down next to the creature and started talking. "Hello. How are you?"

It said, "I'm okay. How are you?"

I was a bit shocked because it had such a sweet voice, unlike the raspy voice in monster movies. I also didn't think that monsters had manners.

"If you don't mind my curiosity, what exactly are you?" I asked.

Through Their Lenses

She answered, "I'm a baby girl."

I shook my head and said, "I know you're not a human. You started off as a T-rex, then turned into a human, then turned into a green creature, and now you're a human again. If that's not magical, I don't know what is."

The monster looked surprised to say the least.

She said, "Oh, you know about that."

I said, "Yes, I do, and if you don't mind, can you do it again."

She said, "You can't tell anyone."

I said, "All right!"

She said, "I am a shapeshifter. *I can become anything or anyone.* So pick a creature for me to transform into."

"Oh wow!" I exclaimed. "Wait, you can turn other people into different things! Can I call give you a name? Can I call you Animagus?

"Oh yeah, I love that name."

I said, "So, if you wanted to, you could turn me into a tree! Please don't turn me into a tree!"

At this, Animagus burst out laughing.

"I like you," she said. "You're funny. Now what do you want me to turn into?"

"Hmm, a mouse," I said.

"All right," Animagus said.

Then she turned into a mouse. I was expecting shooting stars or something, but she just turned into a mouse.

"Wow," I said. "You transform inconspicuously so that nobody knows about your power."

Animagus said, "I mean yeah! If I had a big show, everyone would know, wouldn't they?"

Just when I was about to ask another question, her stomach growled.

"Why don't you come home with me? I can get you some food," I offered.

"You are very kind. Thank you. And while we are at your house, you can ask me questions. I'm sure you have a lot." Animagus giggled.

"I do." I laughed.

In the back of my mind, I was thinking about how mad my parents would be if I showed up with an animal. I thought, *Well, joke's on them.* I can ask her to turn into a tiny creature while at home and anything else while playing. Just then a question struck me. Animagus seemed worried when I told her about how I knew she had powers. I wondered what had happened. I needed to ask her. Not yet but at the right time.

After Animagus had eaten her fill, we headed to my room. And I started to ask her some questions. I couldn't stop myself.

"Animagus, why were you with a dinosaur?" I asked.

"Oh that. I turned myself into a dinosaur. I figured that it would be easier to find food," she answered.

"Smart. Then why did you pick me up, if you don't want people to know you have powers?" I inquired.

"Sometimes when I'm being an extinct or mythical creature, I get too much into the character and forget who I really am. Oh also, I was being the dragon because I realized what I was doing. I needed to stall, so I wouldn't eat you. I decided it would draw your attention away, so the 'dinosaur-me' could disappear, and then when you were wondering where the dinosaur was, the 'dragon-me' would disappear."

I was totally enjoying knowing the details of how she shapeshifted. I asked my most burning question next. "Why were you so worried when I told you I knew about your powers?"

Animagus let out a deep sigh and said, "I once met another human. I told her about my powers. She wanted to take them. She built a machine to control my mind, so I would do her bidding. Have you learned about the wars in school?

Those wars were caused by her. She made me change their minds with my powers, so they would want to fight. Every single war happened because she found me and used me."

I stared with my jaw wide open. When I could finally speak again, I asked, "Why would she? What would she gain?"

Animagus said, "She is a monster that feeds off people's misery, sadness, and grief. War causes all of that. If she doesn't get any, she disappears. Got any other questions?"

"I do. Why are you being my friend when you couldn't trust any humans?"

"You saved me when you could've been escaping. And for that, I am grateful. Besides I have a good feeling about you." Animagus smiled. And I smiled right back.

What I thought in my head was, *Hmm, my parents said I couldn't have a pet, but I found a shapeshifter as a pet. He can be a million different pets in one. How cool is that?*

What I felt in my heart was that even the scariest of beasts can be tamed with kindness.

Heir

Alita Sebastian

"What are you doing in your bed? I woke you half an hour ago!" Mom ripped off the covers.

Thud! Nyra fell to the ground.

"What time is it?" Nyra groaned, rubbing her back.

"Time to go to school! Get up!"

Nyra got dressed hurriedly. After grabbing her backpack, she headed out the door.

"Mom, I already see the school bus!" Nyra hollered.

"Okay, bye! Have a good day at school!"

As Nyra ran up to her friends, Kathie exclaimed, "Wow! We got here before you!"

"Yeah, my mom woke me up late today."

Nyra lined up at the bus stop. They got onto the bus and sat all the way at the back. She expected the driver to yell at them like he always did, but today he didn't.

Kathie must have thought the same thing and said, "Maybe Mr. Torres didn't see us come yet? Or maybe he thinks that we deserve this seat?"

"He always finds us though," Ava whispered, squinting. "Is it just me, or does Mr. Torres look different?"

"No, I see it too. That does not look like him!"

"Did we get on the wrong bus?" Kathie asked worriedly, hugging her backpack tighter.

"No, I don't think so."

"Okay, y'all, get ready for the ride," the driver announced.

"Wait, that's it? No speeches? I hated those speeches!" Nyra said.

The bus squealed as it started along the road. Nyra stared out the window. She looked for the heart-shaped bush they always passed by. But she never saw it. Kathie and Ava were too busy blabbering to notice.

Nyra turned to face her friends. "We're not going to school the same way we always do."

"Oh, that's strange." Kathie bit her lip.

"Kathie, it's no big deal. Don't be such a scaredy-cat," Nyra retorted.

The bus jolted to a stop. Nyra's face slammed the back of the seat in front of her.

"Whoa! Are you okay?" Ava asked.

"Ow! No, I'm not! It hurts a lot. That driver can't even drive!" Nyra whined.

"You look fine. Plus, you should've worn your seat belt," Ava said.

The driver got up again. "This is your stop, and everyone has to get off! I know usually you go to school, but today is a special day! Enjoy your new home!" He laughed hysterically, shoving the first row out of the bus.

Kathie started to panic. "We can't get off here! How are we gonna get to school? Or back home!"

Ava hugged her. "It's okay, Kathie. Calm down. We'll figure this out."

They walked out of the bus. The town looked abandoned. There were dead plants near every house. The lawns were all tan and yellow. Broken refrigerators, washing machines, and dishwashers were scattered around each house, and the paint of the houses was scratched off.

"Who even lives here?" Ava asked.

"Why, we do, of course," a voice behind them said.

All three of them jumped up and screamed. Then they ran into an old schoolhouse, with their classmates right behind them.

"I am never going out there again!" Kathie cried.

"Kathie, I know you're scared, but right now we have to figure a way out of here," Ava said, sitting in a chair, still panting.

Nyra stood on a desk. "Okay, people. This is definitely not what we planned, and I know some of you are scared. Too bad! Start splitting up and look for a nearby bus stop, a library, or another town!" She got back down.

"Let's go find that library!" Nyra said, heading out the door.

Nyra decided to look on the cleaner side of the town. They all went into every building.

"Okay, we need to ask someone for help. This is going to take forever," Ava said.

"Are you looking for something?" a familiar voice said.

It was the same lady as before. Nyra quickly turned around.

"I didn't mean to scare you the other time. It's just wonderful to have visitors," the old lady said, smiling.

"Oh, it's fine! It's nice to meet you! I'm Ava, and these are my friends Nyra and Kathie!" Ava said.

"We actually got stuck here. We went on the wrong bus, and it led us here. We really need to get back home, but we don't know how," Kathie whispered, still hiding behind Nyra.

"Do you happen to have a library here?" Nyra asked.

"I'd be happy to show you the library! This way!" The lady walked toward a tattered building. It was bent like a palm tree. "Here we are! Have fun!" The lady disappeared behind the building.

Nyra walked in. Behind the doors, it was a totally different place. There were millions of shelves filled with books, and the corners of the shelves were coated with cobwebs.

"It's bigger than I thought," Ava said in awe.

They all looked around, checking every aisle.

"There! The history shelf!" Ava said as she pulled out a giant book.

Nyra sat beside her. They opened the book to the table of contents. There were pages and pages of information. One of the chapters was labeled: "Our Town's History."

"This must be it." Nyra flipped to the chapter. She expected to find more pages of information about the creepy town, but she found nothing.

"Where's the rest of it? Someone ripped out the pages!" Ava pointed at the remains of the pages. She placed the book back.

Ava looked around. "Wait, where's Kathie?"

"She was right here. Oh, well, let's just go back and see what the other people found,"

"But, we can't leave Kath—"

"Relax, she'll probably be waiting outside. She's just being a coward," Nyra said.

They walked back to the school. There were a lot fewer people, and they were empty-handed and as clueless as ever.

"So did you guys get us anything?" Nyra demanded.

"Nope! We couldn't find anything. There's no record of any towns nearby,"

"What? You guys probably didn't even look properly! Look, I need to get out of this place," Nyra spat out.

"Nyra, we all have to get home. We're helping as much as we can!" Ava said.

"Do you want to get out of here or not?" Nyra glared.

"Yes, of course I do. But maybe…" Ava's voice trailed off.

"That's what I thought." After Nyra barked more orders, she went outside to look in the library again.

"Hey, Ava, don't you think I'm a great leader?" Nyra asked. She waited for the answer.

"Ava? Hello?" She turned around, but no one was there. She slowly walked back to the school. To her surprise, some of the boys from her class were there.

"Guys, you're supposed to be with your groups!"

"We're the only ones left from our groups," a boy said as he hid under the table. "The other people just disappeared. We have no idea where they are."

"Ava and Kathie left me, so I'm alone too." Nyra looked out the window.

"Well, I guess walking home is our only option now." She sighed. She noticed a difference in the number of people there were now. There was only the boy under the table.

"Where did the others go?"

"I don't know," he said, shivering.

She felt a chill on her back. She hoped it was nothing and everyone was safe. She hoped they were just working really hard to get out.

"Hello there, why are you here alone?" It was the lady again.

Nyra jumped. "Alone? I'm not alo—"

Nyra searched for the boy, but he was nowhere to be seen. Her classmates had just left her. They didn't even care about how scared she was.

"Have you seen my friends?" Nyra asked.

"Oh, yes. I certainly have. Come with me, Nyra."

"How do you know my name?"

"I know many things. Especially about people."

Nyra cautiously followed the lady into the town. There was a forest at the edge with tall trees covering the dark blue sky. She had a feeling her friends were here. The lady cleared her throat.

"My name is Olga, and I'm the one who is taking your friends. I have been watching you. You are selfish, rude, and absolutely perfect. You are lucky I picked you," Olga cackled.

Through Their Lenses

Nyra was horrified. She ran as fast as she could. All this time, she was just helping Olga. Her selfish attitude was exactly what Olga wanted. She stopped to catch her breath. Olga appeared in front of her. She grabbed Nyra's hand and dragged her back to the forest, Nyra screaming the entire way.

Olga turned back toward her, raising her fist. "You can run, but I will *always* find you."

Everything went black.

Nyra's eyes slowly fluttered open. She found herself chained to a rock and struggled to free herself.

Olga stood in front of her, smiling. "Finally, I have found my heir."

Blood Ties
Gavin Chan

It was April 1861. Charlie Johnson's fading, squat golden carriage cantered down hustling, boisterous Beale Street. The brick buildings towered over the crowds, long white bolts of light bounced off the crisscrosses of ironmongery, and despite the febrile atmosphere, the stores were piled high with tobacco tins, multicolored bourbon bottles, and other decadent delights from the border states. As Charlie's carriage stopped in front of the Johnsons' dry goods store, he jumped off without dusting off his boots, anxious to return to his family. Rumors, nonsense, and even some official statements were spreading rapidly around Memphis. Charlie heard a newspaper boy shout, "President Lincoln angers southern secessionists! War seems inevitable…"

Charlie ran up to his family's apartment, knocking on the scratchy wooden door a little more hurriedly than usual. He remembered the Stoics, like Epictetus, his father had taught him about, and relaxed. The door swung open. Charlie saw his mother with his younger sister on the cracked armchair, looking very anxious, but busying herself with preparing peas.

His mother softly whispered, "It's not safe for us here anymore. Your father and I have decided to move north."

Charlie was lost for words. He had lived in the hardworking border city of Memphis his whole life. And this journey was not going to be as simple as jumping on a train anymore. The family discussed their options long into the night, but no answer came.

Charlie woke up to the sound of hooves, boots, and indeed celebration outside. He suppressed a cough. But as soon as he stood up, his chest heaved, he bent over, and then *it* happened: he coughed up blood. Charlie froze. He heard his family buzzing in conversation downstairs and made a quick judgment call. His answer, his family's answer, came to him in an instant. He wiped his hand, stood up straight, smoothed his creased and baggy white shirt like a flag, and walked slowly and carefully downstairs. He could not tell his family about his illness.

Johnson told his family that he was going away to tell his friends that he was leaving Memphis. He was not actually lying, after all, he told himself. He boarded a tram and headed to the nearest Confederate army recruiting station, a hastily assembled affair. Charlie saw the coming war as an opportunity for escape, for himself and his family, with honor.

The next few weeks were like a Kansan tornado. Across the Southern states, men were pressured, felt pressured, or pressured themselves to throw in their lot with the CSA. Charlie was hurriedly told of his part in the coming conflict, and he was introduced to a man who would change his life, for better and for worse. Within a few nauseating mornings, Charlie would groggily pull on his gray army tunic and cough up a little blood into a hidden napkin. Every morning, he and his comrades were ordered to get dressed and wolf down their hard biscuits and gravy more swiftly. They were to begin a march to Hardin County, where it was reported that Union troops prepared to strike Tennessee. His green company had only heard stories of battle, delivered with little emotion via telegraph.

One day before the march, Charlie was told to report to a certain captain with a cigar. His slaves were cooking him lunch. Charlie walked to the tent and met a pointy-bearded, dark gentleman in a long gray "ivy-sleeved" army tunic and civilian's soft wide hat. He stared at Charlie for a beat, only to shift unnervingly to gentlemanly tones and tip his hat, introducing himself as Mr. Donelson McGregor the Fourth. Charlie handed him the cigar tin, and the conversation turned to the South. Going on a quiet little rant, McGregor told his standing soldier that, whatever some pretentious and sentimental Connecticut housewife might think, Africans needed Europeans to govern them. He also explained to him how he treated his slaves fairly and equally. Johnson's passions were aroused, as he had no love for slavery, though he had had cause for little extended conversation with negroes before now. As far as his simple moral sensibilities were concerned, owning any person, whatever their personal qualities, was wrong; that was all he and his family had quietly decided on beforehand.

With studied gentleness, a slave then came into the tent, carrying a hot cup of tea, but this was a new environment for the house slave to work in; suddenly, he tripped over a stone on the carpet, and the porcelain teacup came crashing down onto Charlie's lap. McGregor yelled at his slave without even bothering to use his name and grabbed a short rope he had under his chair. Unsatisfied with mere rebuke, he then whipped the slave outside, making him fall to the ground in muffled pain. Charlie was disgusted at himself, as he had no choice but to stand to attention in his officer's tent. However, he also suddenly had an idea, which was both generous to his peers and would help him achieve his ultimate goal.

Finally, one ruby-red dusk in Hardin County, Charlie and his company slowly snaked out into the forest surrounding the Union army's tents. McGregor lay down with his rifle, aiming slowly and coldly at a black cook outside the white officers' section. *Boom!* The first shot of the Battle of Shiloh was fired. The cook's body fell to the ground and—Johnson saw this for the first time—blood foamed on his chest as he noisily writhed on the patchy grass. Charlie felt repelled by the sadism of McGregor, as Union soldiers realized the Confederates were there, and those at the back of the camp quickly sprinted to their cannons. Suddenly, chaos erupted as smoke came from all directions, and soon all Charlie heard and saw were the screams, shouts, and charging bodies of men in every direction. Bullets whizzed around Charlie's head as blue and gray bodies collapsed like sacks of potatoes, falling to the ground in the forest clearing around the tattered tents. Charlie ran away from the pandemonium, but a big square figure emerged from the smoke and grabbed him by the shoulder. Charlie recognized the gray Confederate captain's uniform and the tall hat, but more importantly, he recognized the furious eyes and black beard. It was McGregor, not about to let one of his lambs stray from his flock.

As night fell, McGregor explained to the shell-shocked Charlie that nearly all the men in his company had died when a bomb exploded in a tunnel near their trench; their charge on the Union camp saved the lives of those who were not kept in reserve. At the mess, the Confederate soldiers ate dinner quietly, despite their exhaustion and need for meat; they were so young and green that they dared not address the carnage that had unfolded. They chewed their stale bread in the end and tried to prepare themselves to clear the battlefield within a few hours of fitful sleep.

As he left the mess, Charlie then realized that now was the perfect time. Yes, time to steal McGregor's slaves and arm them for a run to the north. When Charlie was sure that all of the Confederate soldiers were asleep, he quietly slid down a grassy hillside toward the negroes' simple quarters. He unbuttoned the house slave's tent and crouched down, whispering to the slaves inside, telling them to go out of the tent and follow him to the arsenal to grab shotguns and rifles. He handed them out to each of them, and with a glint in his eye that no acquaintance of Johnson had experienced beforehand, told them to run north with him over the chewed-up battlefield to freedom. Their hearts pounding, the men sprang to their feet, especially the scarred one, Peter.

At dawn, McGregor went to check on Charlie, only to realize he was gone. McGregor had been too gentlemanly to act on his instincts and lock Johnson up before; now he cursed his magnanimity. McGregor immediately shouted, "Johnson has deserted!"

Across the camp, whatever young men there were, with whatever energy they had left, threw on their boots, felt a rush of angry blood, and joined their master and commander to punish this vile coward. Within minutes, McGregor and his other green grays started chasing Charlie through the battlefield; and McGregor was repelled to see the blacks, too, armed, firing wildly behind them as they ran like hares over the craters and metal debris.

Charlie and the slaves knew a marathon awaited them as they heard the shouts and wild shots approach. At the other end of the Shiloh slaughterhouse-field was an abandoned farmhouse. Charlie and his comrades made for it. If he was to die, Charlie thought, better here than beneath his mother's tears.

McGregor pulled out two pistols and started firing, more inaccurately this time, on his foes, black and white, while the company scattered over the broken field toward the farmhouse. In his rage, McGregor could not even look beneath his filthy boots. He climbed over the lip of a crater, tried to shove aside a broken barbed-wire fence, and succeeded only in tripping over a corpse into a neighboring crater. With a final, piercing cry, he impaled himself on an errant bent iron stake at the bottom.

Charlie dived through a broken door into the farmhouse with his comrades, clicking his shotgun into place. It was going to be a long and ruthless run to freedom, but he could probably get it done before coughing up the last of his blood—and releasing the last of his blood ties.

Through My Lens
Mridula Srinivas

A dream is a fragile thing. It can break or shatter in a matter of moments. It can be fulfilled with the tiniest margin of luck. Anything can change its course or path, as you treat it as the most important thing there can be in this realm.

The Hillwood Square Garden, filled with lush colors and a scent of fruit, could be described as an area of pure heaven for botanists. However, not everything is so black and white. The Hillwood Square Garden, with rows and columns of sunset-colored roses, could be a realm of envy. The flowers could bring forward feelings of loathing and jealousy, from botanists gazing upon flowers more beautiful than their own.

A tingle of excitement courses up my veins every spring. After all, the flowers would be perfect to look at through the lens of a camera.

My dusty case, covered with dust, looks ordinary enough. However, inside, the dreariest of containers holds the most precious treasure of all—my camera. In my opinion, smartphones with their small cameras are an artificial way of capturing one's true perspective.

However, I would be gladly willing to use my cell phone right now, I thought as I absorbed the scene in my head. Lively music echoed through the fields, as the savvy tunes of a flute flew by. The sounds couldn't be captured by a camera, but the feel of the moment could. The flowers seemed to perk up as the sun grew brighter, creating a lovely light to capture the essence of this moment.

I rolled my wrists and gently attached my classic Nikon Z50 to my wrist, using the metallic strap. Its rotation functions worked perfectly as I held the camera up to my eye. The scene that came to life right before me truly showed me my love of photography. Seeing it all come together perfectly created a sensation that would help me create many more marvelous moments like this.

My love of photography originally developed during my school days. As a child, I used to be bullied...a lot. When I finally learned that hiding behind the bushes wasn't enough to stop the blunt words from cutting through me like sharp blades of ice, I knew I needed something different. I wanted to dissolve behind a camera forever. I would be an observer, but not a part of the final production.

Through photography, I could be valued. I could see color, texture, and volume come to life while hiding behind my camera. I wouldn't have to speak or engage. Just make sure everything else is perfect. After all, there's a lot more to photography then you would think. In order to get the composition of the photo perfect, the subjects in your photo should be positioned properly. Everyone should be sure of the type of photo they would like to be part of. Most importantly, the whole ambience of the photo should click. No pun intended.

In the garden, right as the perfect shot came alive through my lens, a blonde figure stepped forward to the right of the camera. She changed my view, and the moment was lost. The photo clicked, but it wasn't my vision. My hopes went right down the drain, as I immediately tried to move, craning my neck to see if I could position the camera somewhere else.

"You're very serious about photography I can see. You didn't even let me apologize for cutting through your picture," an amused voice spoke.

I looked up to see a blonde woman smiling at me. She had a cuddly Pomeranian in her arms.

"I didn't mean to seem rude; I was just making an effort to capture these beautiful flowers with my camera," I proclaimed, looking for an opportunity to get to the side of the pasture.

"No harm done. I'm Angela, manager of the warehouse. I pop by the gardens every once in a while to see how the flowers are thriving. I've been coming here more often lately, and I see you a lot. You always have a focused look, taking pictures. I'm inquisitively asking, what's your goal?" she spoke quickly, properly, and seemed to take a genuine interest in my passion. I was taken aback. No one really wanted to know the magic behind the show.

"I travel a lot for photography, and everywhere I go, I try my best to take a shot that captures the feel of that moment in time. The perfect shot, some might call it," I admitted.

"And what would you say gets incorporated into a perfect shot?" Angela shot me a thoughtful look as she scanned the meadows. "This place is very perfect to look at, but there must be a spark or a certain idea that gives a whole new meaning to a picture."

"You're right. For me, it would be capturing the essence of the moment. Capturing the subject is not enough. You have to grasp the feel of the moment. That's what I think anyway."

"I really feel what you're saying. This may surprise you, but I have a genuine interest in photography. The special something for me, that makes my pictures perfect, would be the experience. For example, I took some great snaps in the Alps. However, I couldn't seem to make the pictures amazing until after I experienced snow-trekking and snowboarding. Once I did, I could see the pictures come to life."

"That makes sense. It's all about perspective in a way. You take a better picture if you can relate," I added thoughtfully. "Anyway, like I said, I managed to get one click with you featured. I can print it for you if you like."

I rushed to print out the photo and put it in an envelope. Angela's eyes widened at the sight of the photo.

"It's amazing. I really love it. Thank you for this," she gushed as I sighed. "I sense you're not happy with it?"

"It's not that. But every picture I take has to have a theme and a spark. This one looks ordinary. Nothing special. I appreciate it though."

"Regardless of what you think, I love it. Well, that could be because I love the dress I'm wearing. And Rocky looks so cute." She laughed and cuddled her dog, who was barking ferociously at me. "Thank you for the picture. Hope everything works out. Bye!"

As she walked away, I felt dazed. The picture had not come out with that effect I had wanted it to. However, Angela had adored it. Considering she loved photography, couldn't she tell the lighting was off? Couldn't she tell the position was off as she was a bit too close to the camera?

Maybe she could not tell because it was her. Her and her life, I thought. *Her dog. Her life. Her experience.*

My photos are taken by me, but don't show anything about me. I always try to capture the perfect photo, but not one that works for me. Maybe I'm the missing element. My photos should reflect my personality.

That idea came to light, and it felt right. It felt like the spark I needed.

After whipping out my camera, I smiled next to the flowers. I didn't worry about the lighting or the background or how I looked. I just smiled, feeling happy to be able to capture a beautiful moment with these sweet fragrances around me.

The picture wasn't perfect through everyone else's eyes. My makeup was patchy, some of the flowers in the background were old, but it didn't matter. Through my lens, everything was perfect.

Home

Aydan Wong

"Girl! Get over here, now!" a voice called.

Alexandra recognized the shrill, piercing words as her stepmother's. She sighed, then got up from the ground and slowly started walking. She looked up at the towering gray mansion in front of her and was suddenly filled with sadness as she remembered her father. He had married Ms. Calabaugh after Alexandra's mother had died, when she was seven years old. At that time, Calabaugh had been nice, sweet, and civil to her. But not two years into the marriage, Alexandra's father had died suddenly of the flu. Calabaugh had acted so sad, so dejected for the loss, but Alexandra didn't buy it. She suspected that her stepmother was happy that her husband had died, for she was greedy. Sinister.

As soon as Alexandra's father was gone, Calabaugh took his money and made Alexandra a slave to her word.

Alexandra looked to her right, where a big bronze gate with a huge lock stood. That gate had come with the house, her father had once told her. There was no key, so it wasn't important. End of story. It had been that way for as long as she could remember.

Alexandra stepped into the house, bracing for punishment.

"Girl!" Calabaugh barked, tiny droplets of spit falling onto her brow.

Alexandra refused to wipe the saliva off, refusing to give this woman the satisfaction.

"Look at me when I'm talking to you, girl!" Calabaugh shrieked. Her voice got dangerously soft. "You wouldn't want to spend another night in the basement—" She paused, leaning closer. "With the rats?" she finished.

"No, ma'am," Alexandra murmured, looking down.

Calabaugh smirked, then aggressively grabbed her hand to pull her to the basement.

"And no supper for you!" Calabaugh shouted as she slammed the basement door shut.

Alexandra shivered. It was frigid and pitch-black down here. Who knew what was lurking in the darkness? Watching her. Waiting for the right moment.

She tried to push unwelcome thoughts out of her head as she carefully lay down on the hard ground. As she started to drift off, Alexandra couldn't help but think of her father. What would he think of her now? Lying on the floor of a basement. Tiny insects crawling into her hair. Rats scurrying around her. What would he think of his daughter?

Alexandra's eyes fluttered open. She rubbed her face. Was she still dreaming? She was lying on a patch of lush green grass, tall stalks towering above her, shading her from the sun. Alexandra shook her head. This couldn't be real. When she pushed herself up from the grass, she gasped.

Hundreds of trees, bushes, and flowers of all colors, shapes, and sizes surrounded her. To her left, she heard chatter from a village consisting of small, oddly shaped cottages. Birds with vibrant colored-feathers circled above her. A butterfly with rainbow wings gracefully swooped in an arc in front of Alexandra and landed on her nose.

It was the most beautiful place she had ever seen.

But before she could step one foot farther into this gorgeous paradise, Alexandra felt a tap on her shoulder.

"Aaaugh!" she screamed, whipping herself around to reveal who had scared her half to death.

"Terribly sorry, miss!" a tiny voice said.

Alexandra looked all around her, but couldn't spot any sign of who had spoken.

"Down here, miss!" the same voice said.

Alexandra looked down, confused. There stood a tiny, strange little creature, looking right back up at her.

"Who are you?" she inquired. The thing looked like a lizard of some sort, except that it was standing on two legs, and was dressed like a gnome!

"My name is Noodle!" the lizard said, smiling and doing a little happy dance. This had to be the most adorable thing she had ever seen. She couldn't help but smile as the creature did cartwheels and waved its stumpy little arms in the air.

"Why hello there, Noodle!" Alexandra giggled, crouching down to get a closer look at him.

Noodle stopped dancing and jumped up on her knee.

"Are you Alexandra, miss?" he asked, his huge eyes widening.

"Erm...yes..." she said.

Noodle shrieked, tumbled off Alexandra's knee, and landed face-first into the grass.

"Oh no! Are you all right, Noodle?" she said, gently turning him around to put him back on his feet. To her surprise, Noodle was smiling.

"Whoo-hoo!" the lizard cried, jumping up and down.

Alexandra was puzzled.

"What's wrong?" she asked, scratching her head.

"What's wrong? What's wrong?? Miss, nothing's wrong! In fact, everything is right!" Noodle announced.

When Alexandra still was silent, Noodle said, "Terribly sorry, miss! I had forgotten that you don't know!"

"Know what?" she said. "What in the world is going on?"

Noodle motioned for her to follow him, then started running toward the village.

"Wait!" Alexandra shouted, struggling to keep up with the lizard. For such a tiny creature, he was incredibly fast! She didn't catch up with him until they had reached the village. Alexandra gasped for breath. Out of the corner of her eye, she spotted someone coming toward her.

"Hello!" the person said. "You must be Alexandra! Welcome to Bluewern."

"He-hello. Nice to. Me-meet you," Alexandra said, struggling to speak.

"My name is Fenon. Come, child, I will show you around while you catch your breath," Fenon told her, walking to a cottage that had a roof decorated with pink straw. She nodded gratefully, then started to follow him.

"Welcome to your new home!" Fenon said, opening the door to the cottage "We have a shared kitchen in the center of Bluewern village, so that—"

"Wait!" Alexandra cut him off. "What do you mean, my new home?"

Fenon looked at her, deadly serious.

"Alexandra. You mustn't…"

She stared at Fenon, confused.

"Mustn't what? What is it, sir?" she asked. Suddenly, the ground underneath the cottage started rumbling. The walls around Alexandra started turning into dust.

"Aaagh! What is happening??" Alexandra yelled, looking at Fenon for help.

"I fear our time here is ending, child. You must find the key. Speak our name. You will finally be home…" he said, reaching out to her. Then he was gone.

The world turned black.

When Alexandra came to, she was no longer in Bluewern. She was back in the cold basement she had started in. Was her whole experience in Bluewern a dream? The door to the basement opened. Calabaugh stood at the top of the basement stairs, glaring at Alexandra.

"Girl! The floors must be mopped this instant!" her stepmother yelled. She turned sharply to walk away. But before Calabaugh was completely out of view, Alexandra caught a flash of gold.

There was a key hooked to Calabaugh's belt.

Alexandra suddenly realized what she had to do.

"Go, child…get the key…" a voice whispered from the shadows.

Alexandra yelped, then stood up quickly to return to the house.

While Alexandra was doing all the chores her demanding stepmother had told her to do, she came up with a plan. She would wait until Calabaugh was asleep, then take the key from her room.

Alexandra waited in her broom-closet-size room for Calabaugh to fall asleep for two hours. When her stepmother had finally drifted off, Alexandra poked her head out of her room. Carrying a candle, she crept to Calabaugh's room, trying to be as quiet as she possibly could.

Alexandra slowly opened the door to the room, then winced when it made a creaking sound. Luckily, her stepmother didn't stir. She looked around the room and spotted the golden key on Calabaugh's nightside table. She carefully took it, then snuck out of the room. Alexandra tiptoed down the wooden stairs and opened the front door.

The bronze gate was there, waiting for her. Alexandra walked up to the gate, pushed the key inside of the keyhole, and...frowned. The key wasn't turning.

"No, no, no!" Alexandra cried as she desperately tried to get the gate open. It wasn't budging.

A single tear fell down Alexandra's face. Bluewern was the only place where she felt like she belonged. Even though her experience there had been short, it still felt like where she was truly meant to be. Now, she would never see Noodle or Fenon again. She would be doomed to a life of sleeping in the basement and serving her stepmother. The thought of it all pained her deeply.

Suddenly, she remembered something. Fenon had said, "Find the key. Speak our name." Did that mean something?

"Bluewern," she told the gate. Nothing happened. Alexandra bit her lip. Why would she have thought that was the answer? Sighing sadly, she turned away from the gate. Then, as if on cue, she heard a scraping sound. She turned around, confused.

The key in the gate had magically turned by itself! Alexandra pushed the gate open, and color and beauty welcomed her on the other side.

She sighed in relief, smiling as Bluewern called to her, the birds singing, the plants dancing in the wind. She couldn't explain it, but somehow, this place felt more real than anything she had ever experienced before. She closed her eyes and took a deep breath. Alexandra looked up, her eyes glistening.

She was finally home.

The Prophecy
Bella Marciano

Prologue: Fairy Counsel (Wishtopia)

The five representatives sat around the small rectangular table, each there to work together to make decisions for the five kingdoms, but not doing a very good job of it. They couldn't agree on *anything*!

"Oh, *come on,* you guys!" the head of the fairy counsel, Cosmo Night, said before he could finish taking role. "Can't you just get along for once? The five fairy kingdoms, the kingdoms you each come from, are *relying* on you to come up with a solution. So stop arguing and start working together!"

The five fairies grumbled, but knew this was true. They finalized a plan, and Cosmo had to make it work. He was the only one with magic strong enough to summon the greatest wizard of all time. Because right now, that was what they needed. Not fairy magic, but wizard magic. Cosmo put his palms up to the sky and focused on saying the incantation. He felt the magic running through him. Pointing to a part of the wall with one hand, Cosmo said, "We need a prophecy and a queen."

Suddenly, glowing words in swirly handwriting began to appear as if someone was writing them on the wall with a huge pen. *The prophecy.*

"The Prophecy of the Queen"

You ask, "Who is the future queen?"
It's a girl you haven't quite seen
She will come on the tenth of April
Underneath the tallest maple

I must warn you, the future queen
Will claim the crown when she's just a teen
And if you make the wrong decision
You will lose your queen, if she's without supervision

If the wrong path is chosen, not all is lost
You'll get your queen, just at a greater cost
And maybe the other queen will be better
Time will tell, since you still haven't met her

When she arrives you must take her in,
Show her our life here, her head will spin
And this girl who fell by the maple tree
The future queen shall be: Paisley

***

Fourteen years later

"We've found a way to create another portal," Lily, a
fairy representative, told Paisley. "You're going back to the
human world to find your parents tomorrow! You'll be with an
escort, of course, but that escort will be your best friend, Iris!"

Paisley did not really want to go back to the human world
even though she was tempted to search for her parents.

Twelve years ago, Paisley had been living with her cranky
great-aunt because her parents had disappeared when she was
two. One night she made a wish to find her true family, hoping
to find her parents. Instead, she found herself falling through
a portal that brought her to the tallest maple in Wishtopia. She
was adopted by fairies who told her about the prophecy that
said she would be queen one day. In order to keep her in
Wishtopia, they told her that they were not able to create a

portal for her to go back to the human world. She never thought she would enter the human world again.

When Paisley heard she was going to the human world the next day, she said, "Tomorrow? Why so soon? Can't it wait?"

The fairy council glanced nervously at each other and said, "Oh no! You have to go tomorrow!"

Lily said quickly, "Well, we just want to have you see your family as soon as possible."

Another council member, Serenity, nodded gratefully at Lily and said, "Yes, that's right!"

Paisley had a feeling they were hiding something, and she wanted to know what. Iris, who was being trained to be a fairy council member, may have some information. Paisley just hoped since she was her best friend she would share it.

In the end Paisley agreed to go, and before she knew it, they were floating through the sky on the fairy version of an airplane—a huge dandelion seed. The journey would be about three hours so she decided to ask Iris what she knew before they got to the human world.

"So…" Iris crooned. "Are you ready for your *coronation* next week?"

Paisley twirled her crown in her hands. She'd brought it with her because she had a feeling she'd need it. The fairies said after this trip she'd be crowned queen. She wasn't sure if this trip was a test or what, but something was going on. She couldn't wait to figure out what.

"Yeah." Paisley shrugged, as if bored, and continued. "Well, um, Iris, I wanna ask you something."

Iris looked at her strangely. "Yeah, Pais, what is it?"

Paisley took a deep breath and said quickly, "I know you would only keep a secret from me if you were commanded to by the fairy council, but I *know* something is up about this trip, and I need to know what you're hiding from me. Please will you tell me?"

Iris eyed the crown still in Paisley's hands. "Is that a command, my future queen?"

Paisley, confused by her friend calling her "my future queen" said, "What? Why?"

Iris's eyes widened and she said, "Oh! Never mind, it doesn't matter anyway, really."

"No!" Paisley cried. "Then yes tell me what you are hiding, and that is a command."

Iris sighed and reluctantly said, "The crown was cursed many years ago giving the future queen the power to command her subjects to do anything. It is the monarch's choice whether to use it or not, and that is one reason we don't currently have a queen. We need to find the right one who we can trust and will rule with kindness.

"The other thing I was hiding is that the fairies didn't tell you the whole prophecy. It said possibly due to some decisions made, the fairies will lose you, and there will be another who"—Iris gulped—"eventually replaces you. The dragons are invading right now, and the soldiers are fighting them, but they're not sure they'll survive, let alone win."

Paisley almost dropped her crown. Her adoptive parents, older brother, and boyfriend all were soldiers, and right now they were most likely fighting against the dragons and might even be dead. When she had left, they all had hugged her tightly and looked like they had been close to tears. She had wondered why, and now she knew. She felt betrayed.

"When some of the fairies had suggested you to help fight, the council was concerned this was the 'big decision' that might lead to losing you," Iris continued. "The fairies plan on keeping you in the human world until the war is over, so that you don't die and can come back to restore the kingdom."

Iris sighed, like she was trying to hold back what she had to say next. "Also, when you first came there was a way to get back to the human world, but they didn't tell you to ensure that you would stay in Wishtopia." She then covered her mouth and said, "No, I wasn't supposed to tell you any of that! And...you used your power on me." Iris looked devastated. "The rightful queen wouldn't use it on me." Her voice cracked on the word *me.*

Paisley felt shaken up, shocked, then angry. So terribly angry. How could she become the queen for these fairies when they were going to sacrifice all of the people she loved, without even telling her, to keep her alive? After they had lied to her all these years?

As if knowing her thoughts, Iris said softly, "But the fairies didn't sacrifice your family, Paisley. They're soldiers, and your family chose this for themselves. They wanted to make sure they didn't lose you, and now they won't, right, Pais?"

Paisley felt the anger overcome her, and without really realizing it, with her magic, she lifted up Iris in the air, bound her wings, and said harshly, "Do not call me that stupid nickname. I am your queen and supposed to be your friend. But you kept this from me, so maybe you are not my friend at all!"

Iris's eyes widened, and she whispered, "They *are* gonna lose you."

Paisley narrowed her eyes. "What?"

Iris said sadly, "They're gonna lose you, just not to death, but to darkness." She then added desperately, "But you don't have to let it in you! You can take it back. Just let me back in, and we'll pretend this never happened."

Paisley considered this, but then shook her head and said, "No, I can't do that." Paisley thought a moment. "I was going to drop you, but this will be more fitting."

Iris had given Paisley a friendship necklace, which she wore. Iris's boyfriend was from Tranquility, the water and calming kingdom, so she'd given Paisley a seashell necklace that she'd made the last time she visited there. Paisley had only seen this done once, but she knew she was powerful enough to do this, if she could do it correctly. With a spinning motion of her hand, Iris became smaller and smaller until she was the size of Paisley's pinkie finger. Then, Paisley trapped Iris's soul inside the shell.

"I'm sorry," she whispered as she turned the dandelion around toward Wishtopia, where the fairy council, her family, and her revenge, awaited her.

Fun, Fun, Time to Run
Pranavi Vedula

I scampered through the foliage, the tips of my paws barely scraping against the leaves. I panted as my eyes darted nervously, looking for a spare acorn. Chubbs had said that this was the area where he found his nuts, and Chubbs was the one who always had the most food. He had a keen eye for scavenging for food, and it was evident in his furry little belly. But as far as I could see, there were no nuts, only a few soda cans left over from some distasteful hikers. I clambered my way up an enormous oak tree, the bark gently scraping against my jet black claws.

"Oi! Jabba!"

I could recognize that husky voice anywhere.

"Chubbs?" I narrowed my eyes at him. "You said there were nuts here, but the only things left are trash!"

"Sorry," he said apologetically, and he would probably have shrugged, but he was clutching the branch of a birch tree across from me tightly.

"Well, what is it this time?" I asked him. Chubbs's bushy brown plume of a tail waggled in the air eagerly, as it always did when he was excited.

"I've found so much food! It would last us weeks. Months, even!"

"That's if you haven't eaten it all," I retorted, looking at his bulging belly.

"It's a bit from here, but I promise it'll be worth it," Chubbs pleaded.

Seeing as I had nothing else to do, I followed him.

"Where even is this new place you've found?" I questioned him as we scampered across dead leaves and pinecones.

Chubbs didn't look at me, only at the broken twigs ahead. At last he replied guiltily, "It's a human place."

I let out a shrill gasp. A human place? Everyone knew humans were dangerous! Humans were smart, and they were always looking for new ways to drive squirrels and other "pests" off.

"Chubbs, this isn't worth it!" I exclaimed. "No amount of food could possibly be worth this risk!"

Chubbs sighed. "It's safe, I promise. All we have to do is stay out of sight."

Soon, we reached a clearing in the woods, and it was then that I realized that we were in the backyard of a human house.

"Amateurs. This is too easy!" Chubbs whispered.

I turned and saw he was looking at a pole fastened in ground. Two hooks held two bird feeders, filled to the rim with almost every kind of nut and seed imaginable, even sprinkled with rare pieces of corn. Bird feeders were the cornucopia of our kind, and now there were two real, live ones hanging before me.

"I've been coming here for days now," Chubbs exclaimed. "Watch and learn." He jumped on the pole, shimmied up a bit, and then turned precariously to look at me, expecting some kind of approval.

"But there's plenty on the ground, Chubbs," I protested, poking a piece of corn on the grass with my paw. "We don't need to climb up there."

But Chubbs, who had already turned back, was making his way for the first bird feeder. He shook it a little bit with his remaining paws, and a stream of gold seeds fell into his mouth.

Curiosity burned in me, as the seeds streamed readily into Chubb's mouth. It turned out, climbing up the pole was not as simple as Chubbs made it seem. It was slippery and required a good grip. My paws were sweaty and kept sliding against it. The pole didn't have grooves either, so my claws wouldn't hook into it. Chubbs had just finished and was sliding down the pole casually. I focused on the grains on the ground and eagerly shoved some in my mouth. The sensation filled my mouth, the exhilarating taste of fresh corn and nuts melting on my tongue. It just seemed that there wasn't enough! I hadn't had pumpkin

Through Their Lenses

seed in ages! I relished the taste, relinquishing that savory sensation down my throat, where it rested in my stomach.

"See? I told you it was worth it!" Chubbs declared pompously.

"You were right," I admitted.

Over the next few days, Chubbs taught me the best ways to approach the pole. I learned that if the pole was too hard to climb, you could scamper up the roof of the old toolshed nearby and make a jump for the second bird feeder. Or you could just shake the pole itself, which would release large quantities of seeds. One day though, as I was perched on top of one of the bird feeders, Chubbs looked dismally at the house. It was pea green, with black shutters, and a large wooden deck.

"You know, Jabba," Chubbs told me as I was gorging myself with the pieces of corn, "I wish we could go in there. I've heard that there's even more food. Things like crackers, cookies! How nice would it be to have a cookie instead of pumpkin seeds?"

"Those aren't for us, Chubbs," I reminded him. "We could get sick by eating those."

But Chubbs wasn't listening. "Oh imagine! Crackers with a wedge of cheese, a nice piece of tomato, and maybe just a small slab of ham! A delicacy!" He eyed me. "It's only one trip. I'll never go in again after that, I promise!"

"My grandma told me that there's rat poison and big dogs that like squirrel meat!" I argued.

"Well, your grandma's stupid." Chubbs rolled his eyes. "Follow me."

We stealthily made our way into the house through an open window. It was a hard task getting ourselves up. The inside was strange for sure. Pictures of the humans that lived there were framed on the wall. Everything was so big!

"This is the kitchen," Chubbs declared. There was a stove and a sink, some houseplants on the windowsill, and huge cabinets. The floor was tiled, but some of the tiles were cracking and peeling.

"There's one open here," I told Chubbs, who wiggled his way inside the open cabinet. He squealed in delight.

"What is it?" I asked eagerly, scuttling over to him. I heard a tearing sound as Chubbs started gnawing off the blue packaging of a little box.

"Cookies!" Chubbs squealed. Each cookie was magnificent. They were dark and sugary, with a fat dollop of cream on the inside.

"They're huge," I observed, and turned toward him. "We can split one half and half."

Chubbs began working on his side of the cookie, breaking off little pieces and shoving them in his mouth.

"Mmm!" he moaned. "Delicious!"

I was just about to start my piece too when I heard a noise.

"Go on eat some more. You've already got my cookies!" someone said.

I shot a fleeting look at Chubbs, who was frozen. Slowly, I turned around to see an enormous human staring at me! She had wavy brown hair and was wearing a shirt the color of blackberries. Unfortunately, her expression wasn't as pleasant.

She shouted, "Just you wait. I'm going to call PEST CONTROL, and we'll see where you'll end up."

Fear clouded me. Pest control? We'd heard rumors. Those who had been caught by pest control never came back. I'd never thought I would be in that sort of position. I tried to ignore my heart's loud thumping. The woman found a glass bowl on the counter and placed it over us.

"There!" she thundered. "I'll see how you escape now!"

As soon as she had gone, I started on Chubbs. "This is all your fault! You wanted to come here!"

"No," Chubbs defended. "It's yours. You wanted to come along. If it were just me, I would have been in and out in a jiffy. You slowed me down!"

But it didn't matter. We were still trapped.

"Maybe try and push the bowl over the counter." I suggested. Yet, as much as we shoved and heaved against the bowl, it wouldn't budge.

Chubbs leaned against the bowl miserably. "Only a miracle could save us now."

A miracle came in the form of a little boy.

"Mom! Squirrels!" he exclaimed.

"Don't touch them!" she declared from another room.

"I'll make one my pet," he decided, tipping over the glass bowl and picking Chubbs up in a tiny fist. "You. You're the fat one." He giggled at Chubbs.

CHOMP! The boy screamed and let go of Chubbs, who was racing through his legs. I followed suit.

"I bit him," Chubbs explained. "He called me fat!"

We were racing through the hall when we skidded to a stop. In front of us was a giant monster, a myriad of colors, with pointy teeth.

"Lacy!" the woman called. "Get them!"

How did that monster even have a name? Was this a dog? It had to be! I wasn't worrying about that though! Everything began to happen very fast, as the monster growled, attempting to pounce on us.

"You see a way out?" I screamed at Chubbs. I wanted to kick him so bad now! This was all his fault!

Chubbs whimpered, "There's...a cat flap. But the monster?"

We were chased through tables and under chairs. But the dog would not leave us alone. Gritting my teeth, I began to think of a plan. I scanned the room, and that's when I saw it.

"You big dummy!" I shouted at the dog. "Scared?"

I scampered toward a table near the door but got out of the way just in time for the dog to crash into it. As the woman cursed, I led Chubbs out of the cat flap. We ran frantically, not stopping until we reached the woods again.

"I'm so sorry," Chubbs said, sobbing. "I was so greedy. It's all my fault!"

"It's all right," I said, comforting him. "We learned our lesson."

Tired, safe, but with good stories to tell, we headed home.

Zero

Neer Jain

Hello? Is anyone there? I'll just...oh!

Walking through the brown door on her right, Ada Lovelace saw so many people that her eyes simply could not understand it and so many other things that she could not comprehend. She saw some things she would stuff in her backpack later, and then she saw something else that caught her eye.

Oh, my! I did get some recognition after all!

Hundreds of cardboard slips sat next to each computer, each with dozens of holes in them.

My program! Oh, my lucky stars! Finally, something I can understand here!

Walking over to the back of the room, she saw a very grumpy man, then asked who he was.

"Who am I? I am only Isaac Newton, one of the most famous scientists of all time!"

"Well, if you are so famous, then how come I haven't heard of you?"

"You must have! Newton's laws of motion? No?"

"Oh, yes, come to think of it, I do remember Mother telling me about some snarky man who ended up being super brilliant, but was also quite rude to everyone. Is that you?"

"Humph! Disrespectful!" said Newton. He grabbed a book and walked over to an apple tree to read it.

How...nice, thought Ada.

She walked around aimlessly, then heard an announcement that made her stop.

"Good morning, all. You are here because we are in a pandemic, our worst yet. And they're normally pretty bad."

"Hear, hear!" shouted Alexander Hamilton.

"So, we have decided to bring the smartest minds forward in time to help solve this, by rebirthing each of you so that you can research how each family is reacting to COVID-19, aka the coronavirus. You will meet every Saturday from two to three a.m., and can otherwise communicate through your minds. Any last questions?"

Everyone started grumbling, then one loud voice cut through the general din.

"Hey!" said Hamilton. "How come we have to come back? And where did we come from anyhow? I don't wanna be here. I just heard they released my musical, my *legacy*, on Disney+!"

"You came from the adjacent room, and you were deemed smart and curious enough to be part of this. When this announcement finishes, a backpack will appear on your back, and you can bring whatever you want that is in this room. The backpacks will fit anything of any size. T-minus five minutes."

After a few minutes of general chaos, the voice in the walls said, "Your packs will be invisible unless you need to use them, and there is a ticket inside them telling you everything you need to know. As for your parents, they will be made to think you are their child and you will have an alias. Thank you, and good luck."

Previously invisible gates opened on either side, and everyone rushed out of the room. Everyone was instructed by the same voice to open their packs and see what color train they would be boarding.

Oh, good, Charles is on the same train! thought Ada as she saw her friend boarding the blue train.

She read her ticket, which looked a little something like this.

Train	Name	Age	Location	Hobbies	Friends	Nuclear family	Ethnicity
Blue	Jane Khandelwal	11	Roanoke, VA	Coding, music, reading	Sidus Amica (Charles Babbage)	Mother: Annia Khandelwal, Father: Unknown	Indian-American

Right then, it hit her. She could do so much in this advanced future world, but to do that, she needed to survive, meaning she needed to fix this pandemic. After boarding her train (which she noticed also contained Alexander Hamilton), she found Charles and sat next to him.

"Oh, I'm so excited! How about you, Charles?" said Ada.

Their conversation went on amicably, and before they knew it, they had arrived at their destination.

She had a taxi escort her to her new home, and as she walked through the door, she was overwhelmed by unfamiliar, beautiful scents.

"Welcome home, *bacchi!* (daughter) I'm making idli, and I'm almost done with sambar. How was school?"

Suddenly, the words were on her tongue.

"*Accha tha. Paani?* I'm boiling." (It was good. Water?)

"Sure, sure. All the cups are in the dishwasher."

She walked over to where her new mother had gestured and pulled on the handle—and a cloud of steam shot into her face.

She grabbed a steel cup and got some water. She opened her mouth, then her mother said, "I know what you're going to ask, and no. Violin first."

Well, her mother seemed nice. Maybe this wasn't going to be too bad…

She thought wrong. Ada had come home on a Friday, and it was 1:45 a.m. now. She was still trying to fall asleep, but then suddenly she heard a computerized voice inside her head.

"Your meeting will begin in fifteen minutes."

Well, there was that. She would be seeing Charles in a few minutes. She tossed and turned, and finally, the time came.

"Meeting starting now."

The wall flickered, and Ada blinked. Suddenly, in her mind, she saw many people—everyone who had been on the blue train.

Everyone erupted in response. The mind-call went on for a while, but then she saw a new person join—someone who seemed like they were too old to be one of them.

Who are you? Ada asked.

I am the reason you are here because I am Patient Zero for the coronavirus.

Every person who had been in the medical field began speaking at once, then one person said that Patient Zero meant the first one with a disease.

I have come to help.

What can you do? someone asked.

I know how to solve this, Patient Zero said solemnly.

Ha! You're funny. Guys, if you blink three times quickly, you can turn the call off. I'm out! Ada heard in her mind.

Wait! said the woman.

But it was too late because everyone was already gone.

Well, that helped things, thought Ada after the call was off.

After tossing and turning, she eventually fell into a light, worried sleep.

She woke up in a bad mood. She got ready sluggishly and walked downstairs to find her mother cleaning up the kitchen.

"Breakfast *ke liye kya chahiye?*" (What do you want for breakfast?)

"*Sirf* fruit. Hungry *nahi hoon.*" (Just fruit. I'm not hungry.)

"You can go over to Sidus's for the day. I've checked with his mom."

Ada's mood immediately brightened. She grabbed two oranges, peeled one, and stuffed half of it into her mouth, then said, "Thanks, mummi!"

"That girl will either rebuild the world or destroy it, depending on her mood," said Ada's mother.

Ada ran into the garage for her bike, but then went back inside for her mask.

Once outside again, her mind racing, Ada Lovelace rode over to Charles Babbage's house, where she discussed every single thing on her mind.

Time went on, and the pandemic grew worse. Still, they had no idea how to fix it. Patient Zero did not show up in a call for a month, but that streak was eventually broken. Ada didn't like the fact that the Patient Zero claimed to have an idea. But, one day, Patient Zero finally got them all to listen.

It was Saturday again, precisely 1:57. Ada was waiting for the call to start, and she heard the zipping noise that meant the call would start soon. She got her supplies ready, and Ada Lovelace joined the call to see—

Her.

No.

Not here, not now! How is she still even alive?

Patient Zero was sitting in a swivel chair, trolling the meeting once again.

Hello, all. You didn't listen, so now I'm here to make you do just that.

You all have one thing in your eyes. Everyone read their thing aloud, and maybe one of you can solve it.

I've got a...potato? said Hamilton.

Yeah, I've got a gummy bear, said someone else.

Ada's popped up on the screen. It was a riddle!

If you know what you've been told,
The answer to this is simple and bold.
The first word of the second or third line in this,
Then the first of first and second of kiss.
What word has been repeated in this verse?
The last three letters of it don't go first.
Now, here is your final piece of ev'nce,
Third, second, sixth, of the seventh,
And the last of the third line, sixth word
Will complete most of this, rest be assured
Now, once you solve it, this bit'll be better
"The first letter." Yes, that is all. "The first letter."

Alphabetical, said Patient Zero. *Each person, alphabetical by last name, then the first letter of their hint.*

The team talked for a while, discussing their clues, organizing them, and trying to come up with a solution based on what was there.

Well, we're done for. Not one person can figure out how to do this, thought someone in the group.

Sad agreements came from the rest. Her brain had been swimming in clues and the riddle for the past fifty-five minutes, trying to make sense of "gummy bear, potato, Relenza"—then her brain simply arranged it.

I've got it! she exclaimed. *I know how to solve this conundrum!*

Fin

Ada Lovelace was the creator of the first basic computer code, which was made using a set of cardboard slips with holes punched in them. She was also the first person to imagine that a computer could be used for anything but calculations. She made the code for her friend Charles Babbage's computer, known as the Analytical Engine. She is also known for translating a paper on the analytical engine, written by Luigi Federico Menabrea, from Italian into English, with her own tweaks. She was educated in math by her mother, Annabella Milbanke, and she was fascinated with her father Lord Byron's work, even though she never knew him. A computer code has been named after her.

The Adventures of Super Simon
Yung Wing Sum

One sunny morning, Simon woke up and got ready to go to work at the nuclear power plant. He ate breakfast, brushed his teeth, and dressed. He hurried downstairs and began his daily walk to the plant.

He had taken the job at the nuclear plant because it was fairly near to his apartment. He didn't really care about nuclear energy. It was just a job for him.

A few hours later, Simon was working at his computer station when he suddenly heard an alarm. He asked Arthur, one of his colleagues, what was going on.

"Something is happening in the second reactor!" Arthur yelled, an anxious look on his face.

Simon and Arthur quickly ran to the reactor room to see what was going on. He immediately saw what was wrong. Somebody had dropped their lunch burger into it!

"How do we fix it?" Simon demanded.

Arthur anxiously replied, "The only way I can think of is to have somebody crawl in and pull the burger out."

"I'll do it!" Simon said.

Cautiously, Simon entered the chamber. He reached for the burger—and suddenly fell into the uranium cooling tank.

I'm a dead man, Simon thought. But to his surprise, a few seconds later, his body started to shiver and he slowly rose into the air.

"Wow! I'm flying!"

"The uranium probably mingled with the atoms in your body and is making them float," said Arthur.

At first, Simon couldn't control his flying. Eventually, though, he found he could fly faster and more accurately by holding his body straight like a rocket and holding his arms like a gliding bird.

"You must feel weird! You should take the day off," said his boss, Mr. Liu, with a very suspicious look on his face.

"Thanks!" Simon replied, happy to have the rest of the day off.

On the way home, however, Simon stopped suddenly and asked himself, "Why am I walking? I should be flying. I have superpowers!" He raised his arms high and floated up into the air.

And that's how Super Simon was born.

A few days later, while Simon entered the bank to deposit some money, he wondered if he should start building a team to work with him as a superhero.

Suddenly, a masked man holding a gun yelled, "Nobody move! Show me where the dough is!"

The security guard rushed to the vault. The armed man stood next to him, pointing the gun. "Quicker!" the man demanded.

Terrified, Simon ducked under the table with one of the bank tellers.

"Have you ever been taken hostage here before?" Simon asked him.

The teller nodded and whispered, "The last time, some people tried to hack into the codes of the vault. But I prevented that. I have level-five computer knowledge, so I hacked their computer and I made it go kaboom!"

"What's your name?" Simon whispered.

"Henry," the teller replied. "Why do you want to know?"

"Don't tell anyone. But I'm a superhero. And I think I could use your help. Want to join my team?"

Meanwhile, the robber somehow sneaked away from the bank without anyone seeing him.

How did that happen? Simon wondered.

Everybody crawled out from their hiding places and went home.

As Simon was walking—not wanting to fly and reveal to people his superpowers—a thought occurred to him. Before he disappeared, that bank robber looked somehow familiar.

Two weeks later, Simon was having a delicious fried chicken lunch at KFC with Henry.

"Do you want any superpowers?" Simon asked him while stuffing a piece of chicken into his mouth.

Henry glanced up at him, surprised, with a spoonful of mashed potatoes ready to go into his mouth. "Superpowers? The superpower I have wanted for a long time is super speed. When I was in school, I used to get teased because I ran very slowly during P.E."

"I think I know somebody who can make you super fast," said Simon, licking his fingers. "His name is Arthur. He's a genius who works at the nuclear plant with me. Arthur figured out how the nuclear reactor gave me the ability to fly when I accidentally fell into a cooling pool a few weeks ago. Now, he can adjust the control panel to give somebody any superpower they want. He can also build all kinds of inventions to help us fight crime."

"Wow, he sounds cool and smart!" said Henry, taking a big slurp of his Coca-Cola. "Let's hurry there now!"

"You're faster already," laughed Simon.

Henry headed back to the nuclear plant with Simon. They rushed into Arthur's office.

"We need your help, Arthur. We're building a superhero team, and I wonder if you could make my new friend Henry super fast."

"Please step into the reactor room now," said Arthur, opening a heavy door with the words "DANGER! KEEP OUT! STAFF ONLY!" He continued, "I have reset the control panel to give you the superpower you want."

His body shaking in fear, Henry slowly walked into the reactor room. Simon closed the door while Arthur started up the machine.

Steam rose from the uranium cooling pool, and Henry slowly disappeared into the cloud. Seconds later, the door creaked open, and Henry walked out, looking very exhausted.

"Wow! That was like a sauna in there," Henry said.

"Let's test your superpower," said Arthur. "The circular hallway connecting all the reactor rooms is very long. Let's see how fast you can run around it."

"Okay," said Henry.

He started running in one direction. Two seconds later, Henry tapped Arthur and Simon on their backs.

"How fast was that?" he asked.

"You just ran one kilometer in two seconds," said Arthur, a stopwatch in his hand. "That's pretty fast!"

And that's how Speedy Henry joined Super Simon's team.

As soon as Henry left and Simon and Arthur returned to their office, Mr. Liu suddenly appeared out of thin air. "Little did they know that I was standing behind them listening to their whole conversation," he laughed, rubbing his hands together. "They know nothing about my evil plans, but I know everything they're going to do."

A few weeks earlier, after Mr. Liu told Simon to take the rest of the day off when he fell into the reactor pool, he secretly went into one of the reactors himself and gave himself the superpower of invisibility, a power that turned anything he was wearing invisible, too. But unlike Simon, Henry, or Arthur, Mr. Liu never liked to help other people. He had no family and he had no friends. The only person he ever cared about was himself, Ricky Liu. Yes, you guessed it, the person who robbed the bank without anybody seeing him was Mr. Liu.

Now, Mr. Liu had an enemy: Super Simon. "If he has his own superhero name, I should think of a supervillain name for myself. How 'bout Mr. Invisible?" He went to the Everything Store and bought himself a pair of night vision goggles and some shoes that wouldn't make a sound, and he hid these items on the very tippy-top shelf in a closet in his apartment where nobody would see them. Then he wrote a note to himself on a piece of paper: "Plan: Spy on Simon. Take care of his superhero team. Celebrate by doing evil things. And finally destroy Super Simon."

"Muahahahaha!" he laughed at the top of his lungs, like a good supervillain.

Suddenly, he heard a knock on the door. It was Mr. Walter, the old neighbor living next to him. "Sir, it is the middle of the night, and I am trying to sleep. So please, pipe down!"

The next Saturday, Simon walked slowly to his weekly martial arts class with his coach Joanna.

"You're getting better at fighting," said Joanna enthusiastically. "It's time for you to learn some other attacks and some defensive counters."

They walked out onto the soft mat at the center of the dojo.

"Throw a punch at me!" she said confidently.

Simon used all his force to throw his best punch. But Joanna ducked under him, and in the blink of an eye, she lifted him above her shoulders, swung him by his feet, and threw him on the ground.

"What just happened?" he asked, scratching his head and looking confused.

"You just got tossed!" she laughed. "Want me to show you how you can learn to do it, too?"

Then a thought occurred to Simon.

"Joanna, you could really help me in my work as a superhero by always training me."

"What do you mean?" she asked, looking very confused.

"I've developed superhero powers recently, and I'm putting together a team of superheroes. Do you want to join the team?"

"But I don't have any superpowers."

"Don't worry about that. I know somebody who can give you superpowers. Come to lunch with me and my friends and we'll talk more about it!"

After the lesson, they met up with Henry and Arthur at the Chinese Paradise, one of the best dim sum places around.

"Let me do the ordering. I know the owner," Simon said, looking around and raising his hand to get the waiter's attention. He ordered shiu mai, char siu bao, fried noodles with vegetables, chicken fried rice, soup dumplings, crispy spring rolls, and braised chicken feet. "That should be enough to get the meal started," he said.

"You sure have a super appetite," laughed Joanna.

After they ate, they rushed over to the nuclear reactor with big bellies. They ate so much!

Arthur told Joanna, looking very full and about to throw up, "Please step into the room."

Joanna asked in a terrified voice, "Is this gonna hurt?"

"No, not at all," Arthur replied, though he couldn't look straight at Joanna.

Arthur cranked up the machine. Joanna stepped inside the reactor room. Steam rose up from the vents in the floor.

"Three…two…one…!" Arthur yelled.

Slowly, Joanna rose into the air on the cloud of steam, and a big grin appeared on her face. As the cloud of steam slowly dissipated, she gradually settled back onto the ground. But her grin didn't disappear.

"I feel wonderful!" Joanna said. "Let's see if my superpower works!"

The four went out the back door, where there was a humongous boulder in the middle of a grassy lawn. "Let's see how strong you are," Simon said, laughing. "Try and pick up this rock."

Joanna looked uncertain. But with one hand, she picked it up even more easily than she had picked up Simon during his martial arts lesson earlier that morning. Everybody chuckled.

"Let's call it a day, shall we?" Henry asked.

So everybody said goodbye and went home.

The next day, after his Sunday lunch, Mr. Invisible was in his small, cramped, dark apartment.

"I hate living in this old, shabby box," he said to himself. "Wouldn't it be nice to live in the most luxurious mansion in Hong Kong? I don't have the money, but I know a way to get it!"

He sat down to plan his big heist. By just imagining it happening, he turned himself invisible and headed to HSBC headquarters on Causeway Bay. There were many tall buildings, and the streets were crowded with people. But no one saw him, even when they bumped into him.

He went inside the bank and observed the security guards and their shifts. He learned that they changed guards at two o'clock in the afternoon, and there was two-minute gap when there was no guard on duty. So during those two minutes, he planned to throw a can of laughing gas into the air-conditioning system and knock everyone out, even the guards, for about two hours. That would give him plenty of time to hack into the vault, load his bag with hundred-dollar bills, and make an escape out the back door with nobody seeing.

Back in his apartment, going over his plans, Mr. Invisible laughed loudly and rubbed his hands together. "I have the most evil plan of all time!" he yelled.

Suddenly, there was loud knocking on his door.

"Pipe down!" yelled Mr. Walter.

Just after lunch the very next day, Monday, Mr. Invisible packed his stuff before his big heist. He got a large canvas bag with a zip, his soundproof boots, an M4 assault rifle, and black clothes and a black ski mask to hide his identity when he wasn't invisible.

"Good luck to me!" he laughed, and he headed out the door for Causeway Bay.

At the same time, Arthur and Henry were leaving Pizza Hut in Causeway Bay after having the all-you-can-eat chicken wings lunch special.

"I've got to get back to HSBC now," Henry said. "Those chicken wings were delicious!"

"I'll go in with you. I've run out of cash and need some money," said Arthur.

As they entered the bank, a man got out of a brand-new BMW wearing black clothes and a ski mask and holding an M4 assault rifle. He violently kicked open the door and immediately began firing bullets at the ceiling. Everybody screamed and dived under the desks.

"Gimme all the money you have!" he yelled angrily. There was no guard at this time since it was during the guard change. "Open the door right now!"

With no guards on duty, nobody knew the security code. With his M4, Mr. Invisible shot the hinges off the vault door, which fell with a loud crash. Inside the vault were big boxes of cash with combination locks on them.

"Now, open those boxes and give me the money," Mr. Invisible yelled at the manager.

The manager, shivering in fear, crept into the vault and began punching in the combinations on the boxes that held the money. Then he stepped out of Mr. Invisible's way.

"Where do you think you're going?" Mr. Invisible yelled at the manager. He threw the bag over to the manager. "Put the money in the bag!"

Still shivering, the manager began grabbing fistfuls of money, stuffing it into Mr. Invisible's bag as quickly as he could.

While this was happening, Henry, who was hiding under a table in the bank's main lobby, pulled out his cell phone from the back pocket of his pants and dialed Simon.

"There's a criminal in the HSBC Causeway Bay where I work," Henry whispered. "He has shot his way into the vault and is stealing all the money. Come here, quick!"

"Don't worry," Simon replied. "I'll be right there!"

Simon, who didn't have a superhero costume yet, put on a ski mask to hide his identity. He ran outside the nuclear plant and zoomed into the air. Thirty seconds later, he landed by the front doors of HSBC Causeway Bay.

Simon walked through the door just as Mr. Invisible was about to leave. They came face-to-face—or, rather, mask to mask. Simon stared at Mr. Invisible. Mr. Invisible stared back at Simon. It looked like a world championship of staring contests.

Suddenly, with a snap of his fingers, Mr. Invisible disappeared and dashed away. Simon stared in amazement as the black canvas bag full of money floated out the door.

Mr. Invisible reappeared for an instant.

"You'll never catch me," he laughed. And with another snap of his fingers, he disappeared again and ran out the door without anybody noticing.

Just seconds later, the Hong Kong Police arrived. Guns drawn, they surrounded the masked man standing in the lobby: Simon.

Henry quickly jumped out from under the table where he'd been hiding and ran over to Simon's defense. "No. He isn't the bad guy. The criminal ran away. This is the person who tried to stop the robbery!"

After the police had gone, Simon hung his head and looked at the ground sadly. He had failed in his attempt to be the protector of his town. Simon walked out the door slowly, dragging his feet. He flew home feeling very depressed.

That evening, Arthur, Henry, and Joanna knocked on the door of Simon's apartment. Simon opened the door. He still looked very depressed.

"What's wrong?" Arthur asked.

"You guys should come in," Simon sobbed.

They all sat on the couch.

"I was at the bank when the big robbery happened," Simon said.

Arthur and Joanna gasped. They had heard about it on the news, but Henry hadn't told them the whole story about Simon's attempt to stop it. Henry and Simon filled in the others about the whole incident.

That weekend, Joanna invited Henry and Arthur to her martial arts studio to have a secret meeting.

"I'm very worried about Simon," Joanna said when Arthur and Henry arrived. "Ever since that bank robbery, he just stays at home all day, and he doesn't talk to anybody. So let's think of a plan to restore his confidence. Any ideas?"

Henry stood up, looking excited. "I think we could act out a crime scene, disguising ourselves as the robbers, and make an anonymous call to Simon, asking him to come and help."

"That's a great idea," said Arthur. "I agree."

"I get to be the head robber," Henry yelled with excitement.

"I have a friend who has a convenience store in North Point we could borrow for an hour," said Joanna. "Back in high school, I studied theater, and I can do my own makeup to look like an old woman working behind the counter."

Late the next morning, while Simon was still asleep, his phone rang. He woke up and heard a voice he didn't recognize whispering, "Somebody is robbing a convenience store down in North Point on Cloud View Road. Come quick! We need your help!"

Simon was so excited, he forgot how depressed he'd been feeling. "I'll be right there!" he said.

In a matter of minutes, he flew to the crime scene. Behind the convenience store counter, he saw an old woman, both of her hands raised in the air, and two masked gunmen pointing pistols at her.

"Oh no! It's Super Simon!" both of the gunmen cried. They dropped their guns and ran out of the convenience store.

"Thank you for saving my store, and my life," said the woman. "You're the best, Super Simon!"

"No problem, Grandma," said Simon. And then he flew home, feeling proud that he had finally saved someone.

Meanwhile, Joanna took off her old woman makeup, breathing heavily with excitement. Just then, Arthur and Henry walked into the store, having taken off their disguises.

"Our plan worked perfectly," Joanna laughed. "We really helped him get back his confidence. Let's keep this a secret."

Two days later, Simon was at the sewing store in Admiralty. The seamstress had finally finished with his costume. He gave the seamstress an extra tip just to keep the secret.

Simon happily claimed his costume and whistled while he walked home. He tried on the costume. The costume's colors were blue and purple, and it had a utility belt with a buckle. He also had a blue ski mask (different from the one he wore when fighting Mr. Invisible).

He then got a call from Joanna, and she sounded desperate. She said "Quick! There is a jewelry store robbery down in Central!"

"Okay, I'll be right there," Simon said in a professional voice.

Simon quickly put on his superhero costume and rushed over to the jewelry store.

He found a group of four people stealing jewelry and holding customers hostage. Two of them had weapons, while the other two were loading up the bags with jewelry. One of them had a knife, and one of them had a gun.

Simon strutted closer and closer toward the bank robbers. Two of them looked back at Simon when they were loading up the bags with jewelry.

The two who had weapons approached him and glared at Simon. Simon glared back. Suddenly, Simon dashed over to the left and charged into one of the bank robbers and made him fly into the wall with maximum speed.

Then another one snuck up behind him with a knife. As he was trying to stab Simon in the back, Simon leaned backward and dodged it like he was going under a limbo stick. He then slapped away the knife, and Simon said, "This might hurt!" Simon grabbed his arm and twisted it, and he immediately fell to the ground.

The next person tried to box him. He was getting all pumped up, and he did kicks and punches in the air to try and scare Simon. Simon looked at him like when he was judging something that's embarrassing. Simon didn't look scared or. He immediately spun through the air and kicked him on the head, and that knocked him out completely. The last person looked very scared, and he didn't have a weapon, so he ran off like a small baby.

Then everybody got up and started cheering for Simon!

Mystery on the Murder Train
Jasper Loi

Ryan sat on the train seat, his eyes furrowing as he read the new book he had bought. It was two in the morning, and he had just left work with his sister Eliza and their friends. He was sucked into the book, as if he himself were a character created by Agatha Christie.

The lights flickered, the room falling into eerie darkness. Something tugged on his leg, clutching as if he were its last hope. A scream boomed through the car. He clutched his book tightly, shutting his eyelids, willing it all to be his imagination. The lights came back on a moment later. Ryan opened his eyes, but what greeted him was a body—the dead body of his sister Eliza.

***

Ryan sat beside his friends, feeling the detective's gaze upon him. He stared at his phone, swiping through photos of him and Eliza, reliving memory after memory. He couldn't believe he would never see his sister again, that she was the victim of a cold-blooded murder, that she had left him alone, leaving only John, his best friend, with him. His tears became a river, his eyes the top of a waterfall. He knew the scientists were mistaken, that the Earth wasn't a ball. It was an abyss. A chasm Eliza had fallen into with only his leg to grab, the only stable object she had to keep from falling, the sole thing that could have saved her. But Ryan had ignored her, shrugging it off and willing the tug to be his imagination. And so she had fallen, plummeting into death.

A pat on his shoulder jolted him from his train of thought. "You okay?"

Ryan looked up, finding John staring at him. "Not really…but I know I have to keep calm…for Eliza."

"You're right," John said. "If Eliza were still here, she'd want you to stand up, help her solve this murder, and continue on with your life."

Ryan hugged John tightly. "Thanks. You're the only one I have left."

He eyed the others, wondering which of them was the killer, wondering who had pushed Eliza into the abyss.

It couldn't be John. Ryan knew him and knew that John would never kill Eliza. Plus, if he were the culprit, he wouldn't want people to investigate more—meaning that the only suspects left were Jenny and Daniel. Ryan walked over to them, hoping for clues that would lead him to the murderer. He looked at the two, taking notice of their appearance just in case it could help solve the mystery. Jenny had strands of hair covering the right side of her face, possibly intentionally hiding it from view; Daniel's glasses were cracked, which could have resulted from a mishap during Eliza's murder, unintentionally breaking them.

"Who do you think murdered Eliza?" Ryan asked, hoping for someone to slip up.

"We think it's John," Jenny replied immediately. "John and you were sitting beside Eliza. You were reading while he was just sitting there. How could John not notice Eliza being tugged away! I understand you not noticing since you were reading, but John? Also, he probably hated her for exposing his cheating on that physics test and getting his Oxford scholarship taken away! You should tell the detective it was John so we can all leave!"

"Yeah, you should tell him it's John." Daniel yawned. "Plus, it's my bedtime. I'm sorry for your loss, but I don't want it to lead to *my* loss at the math competition tomorrow."

"Gee, wouldn't want you to lose a math competition," Ryan snapped back. "That's definitely on par with me losing MY SISTER!"

Ryan's thoughts swirled in his head. Was Jenny trying to shift the sight of the detective from her to John and cover up her actions? But ultimately, she did have a good point with John holding a grudge against Eliza. Then again, Jenny and Daniel might hold grudges too. Eliza had stolen Jenny's boyfriend, and Daniel and Eliza had a heated rivalry when they were young. But while those incidents were in the past, Eliza had partially ruined John's future, causing him to lose an amazing opportunity. Could John be the culprit? Had their friendship over the years been a lie?

These thoughts clouded Ryan's brain, but he willed them to the back of his head, concentrating on voices he heard coming from the crime scene. He followed them, wondering whether he would find a clue.

As he neared the voices, he saw the detective talking with a police officer.

"I just spoke with the train driver," the detective explained. "He was the one who turned off the lights. He was conducting an illegal deal to get money for his family, but he isn't the murderer, so it must be one of the other suspects."

Ryan couldn't help but feel sorry for the train driver. He understood what it was like to feel helpless, trapped in a cage while your loved ones suffered, unable to give a helping hand. As he sympathized for the train driver, he realized the culprit must have known about the deal, taking advantage of it and using it to their benefit.

Ryan went back to where the suspects were sitting—he gasped, taken aback by his own thoughts. He had just classed his friends as suspects. When had his view of them turned so dark? And who could have known about the illegal deal?

Ryan knew the key to that last question was the train driver. And so he approached the train driver, who stood opposite from the sus—his friends—hoping the man would give him a clue.

"Is there any chance someone could have known about the illegal deal?"

"Who are you?" the train driver asked, jittering with nerves.

"I'm Eliza's brother."

"How is my…my deal relevant to your sister's death?"

"I believe the culprit knew about the lights turning dark and took advantage of it, so no one could see the murder,"

Ryan explained. "Have John, Daniel, or Jenny been on your train before? Could they have found out?"

"Jenny and John have both been on my train a few times this month, but Daniel's a first-timer. I don't recall any moments where they could have heard about the deal though."

"Could they have overheard you talking about it?"

"Come to think of it, I remember talking on the phone with the drug seller and seeing a shadow running away from the door afterward," the train driver said.

Ryan thanked him and headed back. It had to be Jenny or John, but he still didn't have the exact answer. If he were to figure this mystery out, he had to find more evidence, and fast...

As Ryan went toward the crime scene, he heard the forensic pathologist telling the detective about a jewel he'd found in Eliza's hair. Ryan walked over to them, wanting to take a closer look at the jewel. He stared at it in recognition.

He knew who the culprit was.

"Follow me!" Ryan shouted at the detective. He led them back to where the suspects were. "Jenny, come forward," Ryan demanded. When Jenny obeyed reluctantly, Ryan swiped away the hair covering her right ear in one swift motion, exposing the bare ear beneath it.

"That," Ryan said, pointing at the jewel that had been found in Eliza's hair, "is Jenny's missing earring. Jenny killed Eliza!"

"What?" Jenny's jaw dropped to the floor. "No, I didn't! Why would I want to kill her?"

"Maybe because she stole your boyfriend?"

"Daniel and Eliza were rivals too!"

"Then how do you explain this?" Ryan pointed at the bare ear again.

Jenny was speechless, her mouth trying to move yet unable to spit out her lies.

"Eliza deserved it!" Jenny burst out. "Adam loved me, until that witch tricked him into falling for her!"

Through Their Lenses

"But was killing her really worth it?" Ryan asked her. "You're going to live the remainder of your life behind bars, where you can never be with your family ever again. By ending *her* life, you've also destroyed *yours*! You'll live your life alone!"

"I didn't destroy my life," she lashed back. "It was already ruined. My parents divorced when I was seventeen, leaving me with my mom; afterward, even *she* left me, going to heaven and leaving me alone. All I had left was Adam! And she just had to steal him from me. She took away the one thing I thought I would always have! The one person I had left! The one person that loved me! She took *everything* away from me!"

Ryan stared at Jenny, feeling sorry yet also resenting her for murdering Eliza. She had felt betrayed by everyone—but that still wasn't an excuse to destroy others' lives just because yours had been destroyed.

The police officer arrested Jenny, leading her to her remaining life behind bars.

Ryan stared at the train, overwhelmed by the events that had occurred in the last twenty-four hours. He walked toward the crime scene once again, knelt alongside Eliza, smoothed her hair one last time, and whispered, "Goodbye forever…"

Together

Brenna Nichols

I awoke in the middle of the night to the sound of raindrops pounding on the roof. I hadn't been able to sleep very well since the death of my parents.

Their death still stung me as if it were fresh, but I shoved any thought of that aside.

"Don't think about that," I scolded myself.

I had told myself that a lot lately. I had taken every thought, every memory, every reminder, and placed it in the back of my brain, where I wouldn't think about it. My great-aunt Marci had told me that I was denying their death, pretending that it hadn't happened.

"No," I had argued, "I'm just trying to forget it."

She had smiled at me sympathetically and had gone back to making dinner.

Now as I lay awake, staring into the darkness of the room I was forced to call mine, I wondered if maybe she was right. Realizing that my throat was extremely parched, I silently got up and tiptoed to the kitchen for a glass of water.

That's when I heard it. A quiet voice, barely a whisper, but there nonetheless. I slowly turned around, my heart racing, but no one was there. Thinking I was hallucinating from lack of sleep, I quickly got my drink and went back to bed.

I had just stepped through the doorway when I heard it again. I turned, quickly this time, hoping to find the culprit, but again there was no one. That's when I realized that the mysterious voice was saying something.

"Outside."

Outside? I really didn't want to go outside in the freezing rain in the middle of the night, but since the mysterious, scary voice was telling me to, I thought I had better oblige.

I put on my red rubber boots and neon-yellow rain jacket, which was a bold fashion statement with my purple polka-dotted pajamas. I peered into my great-aunt and great-uncle's room. They were sound asleep.

I tiptoed to the front door, opened it, and stepped onto the big wrap-around porch, careful to close the door behind me. Under the porch roof, I could hear the rain better than I could inside. I realized that it was raining much harder than I thought.

"This is stupid," I muttered to myself. But as I turned around to go back to bed, I couldn't seem to make my feet move. It was like they were stuck to the floor. Suddenly, my feet started moving, but I wasn't in control of where they were going. I ended up walking straight into the woods.

After walking for what felt like ages, my feet finally decided to stop. By then, I was thoroughly soaked and extremely tired. I sat down in the grass, getting my pajamas filthy in the process, but I figured that the rain would wash them off. I leaned my head against a tree. My eyes had almost fluttered closed when I heard it again. The same voice as before, except that this time, it was saying something different than before. It was calling my name.

"*Clara Nightingale.*"

I snapped awake. "What?" I said. "What is it? Who's there?"

Two pearly white, translucent figures appeared out of nowhere. They gave off a dim sort of glow, but it wasn't coming from a flashlight. I probably would have screamed if I hadn't been in the middle of the woods where no one could hear me. Instead I just sat there in stunned silence, my tired brain trying to process the bizarre events of tonight.

First, I had woken up in the middle of the night. Then I heard a strange voice. I had taken a hike through the woods in the rain, and now I was seeing things. The figures were coming closer. I knew I should run, but something was keeping me rooted to the ground. The two figures were close enough that I could make out their features. The first was a male, with perfectly combed hair and glasses. The second was a female, with long, straight hair and freckles across the bridge of her nose. I thought they looked familiar, almost like…no, that was impossible. And then they spoke. And my whole world fell apart.

"Clara!" Mom said, a silver tear glistening as it ran down her face. "How have you been, darling?"

"We've missed you so much!" Dad added, smiling.

This was too much. I broke down into tears. Big, gulping tears. I must have sat there for a full minute before pulling myself together. "How are you here?" I asked. "They told me you were dead!" I started sobbing again. My parents looked at each other wearily.

"Honey," my father began, "this is going to sound crazy, but you have to believe that I'm telling the truth, okay?"

I nodded. I didn't think any story he could tell would be weirder than anything I had seen tonight. Dad took a deep breath and began.

"So, there was this sorceress, and she captured your mother and me to be her slaves, but we wouldn't cooperate. So, she used a spell to separate our spirits from our bodies so that she could control our bodies. She put us in a cage along with some other people who she had captured previously. Eventually, we found a way to escape. While we were leaving, we swiped one of her spell books and found the spell that will restore us."

I stared at him in silence for a few seconds. Then I burst out laughing.

"You're kidding, right?" I said, still bent over in laughter.

I looked up at my parents. Neither of them were smiling. The smile quickly disappeared off my face too. "You're being serious?" I asked.

Mother nodded. "I'm afraid so," she said.

It took me a second to process this. "Give me the spell book," I said suddenly.

Through Their Lenses

Dad literally pulled the book out of thin air and handed it to me. I expected it to just fall right through my hands, but it didn't. I flipped through the pages until I found the right spell.

"Hang on," I said, "this says that for you to be restored, that someone has to willingly stay as a spirit forever and repeat the incantation." I glared at my parents accusingly.

"At least you'll still have your mother," Dad said quietly.

"No!" I shouted. "How do you expect me to live my whole life, knowing that there might have been a way to save both of you, but I could only save one?" I started sobbing again. "I need both of you," I whispered.

"Clara," my mother said gently, "your father isn't just sacrificing himself for me, he's doing it for all of them too." She gestured behind her.

Suddenly, a dozen more figures appeared. I spotted at least two children standing with their parents. One of the figures stepped, or rather glided, forward. He looked like an older gentleman, with big muscular arms and overalls. I guessed that he was probably a farmer. He was twisting a hat in his hands.

"Excuse me," he said, "I'm sorry for eavesdropping, but I couldn't help but overhear what you folks were sayin', and, well, I'd like to sacrifice myself for that incantation."

We all stared at him in shock. "Sir…" Father began, but the old man cut him off.

"There's no use tryin' to talk me out of it, my mind's made up. I don't have a family to return to, and my farm wasn't doin' too well anyway, so I don't have a reason to be normal again. Now, would you please hand me that book, darlin?"

I realized he was talking to me. Numbly, I did what he asked. He took a deep breath and said the incantation. The whole forest was filled with a blinding light…

The next few weeks were a blur.

My great-aunt and great-uncle almost had a heart attack when I showed up at their house at five in the morning with my mom and dad. Then we moved back into our old house, since it hadn't been sold yet. Dad somehow managed to get his old job back. I think they were so happy that he wasn't dead that they let him have it. And I went back to school with a spring in my step and a smile on my face. But, even during all the craziness of trying to get life back to normal, we still held a funeral for the man who had brought our family back together.

Imperfect
Cress Wallwalker

The sun had just begun to rise, gracing the horizon with mystic beauty. It was a mirage of wild poppy blues and snowy whites. At least, that was what Azuria had heard from other Detallians. Sunrises were black, gray, and white for her. She might be seated on a cold metal bench nestled next to a fountain in the square, but she felt as if she were in a dark dungeon.

Her dungeon was acrhomatopsia, a disorder that only allowed Azuria to see shades of black, gray, and white. Detallians treated her as an outcast simply because she wasn't able to see their perfect world of full of color.

She was disowned by her family and disgraced by her village, and food was difficult to come by, hunger eating at her like a rabid beast, tearing at her inside out. Azuria couldn't recall the last time she had eaten something. She glanced up, noting that it was oddly early in the morning, and the streets were mostly barren. Perhaps it was a good idea to attempt to steal some food. Azuria contemplated as she sat. If she was caught, she would surely face punishment.

The prospect of fresh food for her to eat was too strong to ignore. She was only further convinced when somebody stepped out of the front doors of a bakery, holding a fresh loaf of bread in his arms. A flour-dusted apron was hanging from his neck causing Azuria to infer that he must be one of the bakers. She had to hurry, or her chance would vanish quicker than it had appeared.

The baker didn't even see her coming as she ran with all she had, despite hunger clawing at her, and yanked the bread from his hands with the force of a gust of wind. Azuria wasted no time continuing to run. Her feet tore through the dirt. She knew that the baker's bewilderment would only last for a short period.

Proven correct, he exclaimed, "Stop! Thief!" and barreled after her.

He seemed to be quite out of luck, considering that there were few people on the street. Azuria was fairly certain that she'd be able to escape this mess if she ran faster. She could hear the baker's footsteps behind her, as he hastily scrambled to catch her. Unexpectedly, he was faster than Azuria could manage and gained speed quickly. He gripped the back of her tattered shirt and pulled her down with an absurd amount of strength. She gasped when she hit the dirt path.

The breath was knocked out of her, and she found herself unable to move as he pinned her to the ground.

Her chaser scowled and snapped, "You soiled the bread. And let me guess, you're one of those Imperfects. That's the only reason you'd be homeless, isn't it?"

Imperfect was a word that Azuria had heard countless times that sent a spark of pain through her. His words were like a knife slicing through her, each one hitting home.

There were only two options in this situation, Azuria realized. She could make an attempt to run but be caught in an instant. On the other hand, she could wait for this to play out. Being quite the coward, Azuria bit on her trembling lip and decided to await her fate but only after she whispered, "Yeah...I am. Achromatopsia, not like I can help it."

The moment the words left her mouth, a guard happened to stumble across the alleyway. Azuria couldn't see him, considering that her face was still smashed into the dirt, leaving her helpless, but she could *hear* him. His weapons dangled from his belt and clinked together as he got closer.

"I see there is an incident of some sort," came a masculine voice.

"Yes, sir, there has been one. This...disgrace...decided to steal the bread that I baked down at the bakery. She says she has achromatopsia." The baker nodded toward Azuria.

The guard hummed before pulling the baker away from Azuria and grabbing her by the wrists. Azuria almost cried out at the sharp pain that darted through her like a bolt of lightning because of the roughness of his actions.

He stared her down like she disgusted him. The guard said, "I believe it would be wise for me to exile you from the land."

Azuria gasped, never having expected a punishment that was as heavy as this one was. She had seen people in Detallia who hadn't been born with a disorder get away with stealing. Azuria shouldn't have expected anything less from the village though.

"As for you," the guard said while he turned to the baker, still keeping an iron-strong grip on her hands, "what is your name? I will make sure you are praised for your help with this girl."

The baker seemed stunned into silence before he managed to get out, "I'm Dorian Quince."

The guard nodded and strode off, dragging Azuria along with him. Azuria wanted to fight, but she had already wasted her energy on running away. Without food to energize her, she was as good as useless.

Azuria allowed the guard to pull her through what felt like miles of forest. Finally, he tossed her down in the middle of an empty field. She grunted as her body rang with pain once she hit the ground. She wanted to call for help, but she couldn't bring her lips to move. All she heard was her echoing thoughts of regret as her world spiraled further into darkness. Azuria felt herself approaching unconsciousness, but that was before someone she didn't know pressed a flask against her lip.

"Drink," said a voice. "It's water."

Azuria guzzled it greedily, sighing at the sensation of finally being hydrated. "Thank you," she said once she'd finally gathered the strength to open her eyes. When she saw the person beside her, she went spiraling. "*Dorian?*"

He shrugged, wiping a hand on his dirt-dusted apron and tucking the flask away in his pocket. "It's my fault you're here. Figured I'd help a poor girl out," Dorian murmured.

Azuria couldn't even bother to glare at him due to his last remark. He had given her water, something few people ever did. "Do you...know of any way for me to get to safety? I assume I'm no longer allowed in Detallia," she spoke solemnly.

Dorian pointed into the depths of the forest and explained, "There should be another city through there. It's called Weori. I've heard it's very different from Detallia. The people who Detallia exile live there, supposedly."

The prospect of a place that would accept her simply sounded as if it were right out of a dream. "How far away is it?" Azuria inquired carefully.

Dorian thought on it, tapping his chin. Then he said, "About three miles. So about forty-five minutes to get there on foot."

Azuria nodded, her eyes glowing. She extended a hand to Dorian, and he gladly helped her off the ground. They exchanged smiles, and Azuria thanked him once more before she began her trek through the forest.

Time passed painstakingly slowly as she neared the brink of exhaustion. The water was enough to keep her going for a little, but not much.

She had begun to think she would never get there by the time she found a cobblestone path leading her into a small, quaint village. Houses lined the streets with occasional carts selling items like flowers and pastries dotting the pathways.

Somebody loosed a small gasp when they saw her. She approached Azuria with curiosity in her eyes before saying, "Ah yes, the typical shredded clothes, definitely malnourished, hair is a *wreck*."

Normally, Azuria would've been annoyed, but she lacked the energy to be. "What do you mean?" Azuria asked.

"Have you been exiled from Detallia?" she asked, voice light.

Azuria was nervous to nod, but she did so anyway.

Her questioner squealed with delight, "Welcome to Weori! We're the people who've been exiled: the blind, the deaf, and the color-blind! We rarely get new citizens; it's a pleasure to have you! What's your name?"

Azuria could tell that this woman was quite enthusiastic first off, but what she had never expected was an entire place full of people who were just like her.

"Azuria," she whispered meekly. "That is my name."

The woman gave her another once-over before beaming, "Come right this way. We'll get you some food and a change of clothes. I think you'll fit in just fine here."

Azuria thought so too, especially as more people rushed to her side to greet her. She learned that day that everyone has a place, no matter how far away it may seem. It had taken her a while to find Weori, but she could tell that the woman was right and that she would fit in perfectly with the other inhabitants.

An Underwater Escape
Alex Chu

As I peer across the water, I can almost make out my little brother on his surfboard, the way it used to be. I gulp, remembering with sadness how I couldn't help him that day he went under. Now I have a hole in my heart. It's something I live with every single day. I can't bring him back, but I feel a connection to him when I am out in the water.

Today, I bounce with the waves and slip on my surfboard, then spread my arms out and regain my balance.

My dad shouts from the shore, "Are you okay?"

I smirk and yell back, "What are you talking about? I'm fine."

After tackling a monster wave, I surf into a pocket and am hidden from the outside world, covered by a deep blue color. In seconds, I escape the wave with no problem and shrug at my dad, showing him I can handle surfing without an issue. I plant my stomach onto the board and swim to the shore.

Suddenly, a force pulls me farther and farther away from my family. The form of a hand tugs me into a hole in the middle of the ocean.

"Jason, come back!" Dad yells.

"I can't!"

Before I know it, I am drowning in the water holding on to my surfboard for dear life. A body that connects to the arm pulls on my foot. I kick at the hand with my free foot, but it is too strong. No matter how much I squirm, I just can't get out of this creature's grasp. Then my body succumbs to the abyss.

I wake up with a headache, enclosed in a glass cage with one side having a locked door. What frightens me the most is the water-filled hallway outside my cage. I bang on the glass, but I pull my hands away in concern immediately, afraid that I might break it and be engulfed in water.

"Get me out of here!" I yell.

Suddenly, two mermen guards equipped with armour and spears swim toward my cage and say, "What do you want, human?"

"Tell me where the heck I am!" I demand.

"You are in Atlantica, the underwater utopia."

"Get me out of here or I'll break this glass and escape."

One guard laughs and says, "If you break this glass, you will drown. Besides, the king himself has retrieved you, so whatever happens to you is his wish."

"Bring him to me now," I say.

A door opens from the end of the hallway, and a merman with long white hair, an angry look on his face, and a long gray beard shows up in front of the glass before me. I can't help but gulp at his massive trident.

With a shaky voice, I say as confidently as I can, "Why are you keeping me here? Let me go!"

"Ha! That is what your brother said when I captured him too."

"My brother?"

Years ago, when I went to the beach with my seven-year-old little brother, I wanted to teach him how to surf. While we were enjoying that beautiful day, my brother got washed far away from shore by the wave. I swam to go get him back, but suddenly he was sinking as if he was being pulled down by something. The truth is we never found him, and I assumed he had drowned, but is the man in front of me the person that made him die? That day scarred me for life, and I think about it every day before I go to bed.

Not afraid of the king anymore, my eyes water and I shout, "Where is he?"

"I've kept him in a dungeon for years here, waiting for him to grow up, so his lungs would grow as well."

"His lungs?"

"Yes. My plan was to transfer his lungs into my body, so I would be able to live on land, but then I thought why not take the lungs of a teenager, someone who has already grown up? You."

"Why do you need my lungs?" I ask, trying to mask my worry that he will actually take my lungs and end my life before I can rescue my brother.

"I am battling my brother Zeus, King of the Sky, to rule the earth, and I must be able to breath above water to rule both the sea and land. That way I will emerge victorious and be the true king of the world."

"You want to fight your brother?" I ask.

"Yes! A battle to see who is the stronger one of us."

"That's insane," I say to him.

"What?" he asks.

"During the years I lost my brother, I was devastated. Not only did disappointment feed on me because I couldn't save him, but there was loneliness as well. I would lie in my bed thinking about my brother who wasn't with me anymore. You would never want to feel like I did."

"Shut it, human. I am going to get your lungs no matter what."

Then he walks out the door and leaves me alone.

I drop down onto the floor and start to sob. I wonder what I can do to save my brother and escape this room, but there is nothing I can do alone.

As I lay crying, I hear a tapping on the glass. I look up and wipe my eyes. It is one of the merman guards, signaling me to come closer.

"Hey, I feel terrible about what happened to your brother and the king's plans, so I'm going to help you escape."

"Wait, that's why you're helping me?" I ask.

"Well that, and I lost my brother too, and I know what it feels like, so I want to help you."

He picks up an oxygen tank and mask and says, "When I unlock the door, you need to put the oxygen mask on right away."

"Okay."

He opens the door, and water starts to flood in. I grab the mask and strap it around my ears to secure it in place. Next, I strap the tank onto my back, and the two of us swim out into the hallway. I ask him if he knows where my brother is, and he gestures at me to follow him. We swim to a series of dark dungeons. I pray that this isn't where my brother has been kept all these years, but I swim along and see a jail-like room that looks just like mine.

Inside is my brother that used to have brown hair, brown eyes, and a cheerful smile. When I see him now, he has the exact same features, but his smile is gone. He looks at me, and his jaw drops.

"Jason?" he says.

"Chuck!"

The guard grabs another oxygen tank and mask stored in the room, and tells my brother the same thing he told me. Chuck nods, and the next thing I know, I am embracing him in my arms, tearing up. The hole in my heart from when I lost my brother is filled again, and I can't stop hugging him. The guard tells us that we must leave soon though, or the king might catch us. He gives my brother and me a strap to keep the oxygen tank on our backs, and we decide to form an escape plan and continue our reunion after we leave. The guard tells us that outside the king's castle is a miraculous world where marine animals and mermaids live together. We then formulate a plan to sneak out the castle through an exit route and swim through the underwater city to reach a portal back to the surface.

We swim through a series of hallways and reach the underwater metropolis. There are many buildings and complexes designed to look like corals. My brother and I take in the huge city, but the guard tells us it is time to leave, or the king will realize we're gone. We continue to swim across to the end of the city, passing dolphins, fish, and mermaids. Suddenly, a booming voice comes from the castle.

I freeze, and the king bellows, "They have escaped!"

The three of us gasp and swim hastily toward the portal now visible ahead. I glance behind us, and it is the king himself, with five royal guards chasing us. We have a lead, but as every second passes, they get closer and closer.

We kick our legs as fast as we can, and I mutter, "Come on, almost there!"

The king is just meters away from us, and we swim through the portal. In just seconds, I am back on top of the water, and the guard is right beside me.

"Wait, where's Chuck?" My voice fills with worry.

We look beneath us, and Chuck's leg is being pulled by the king's muscular arm. I reach out to him, but I am out of breath from tediously swimming out the portal. I am now panicking, and my eyes fill with tears, not knowing what to do.

Unexpectedly, the guard dives into the water and jabs at the king's hand. The king's grip on Chuck's leg loosens, and he is able to swim away, but the king takes the guard's leg instead and tugs him down. He doesn't try to escape though, and he just looks at me, already accepting his fate.

He disappears, and Chuck and I are bobbing on the water with our oxygen tanks, shocked by the guard's sacrifice.

The two of us are relieved after everything that occurred, and we wear half-smiles on our faces. The brother I thought I lost is once again beside me.

Ace of Spades

Rylee Yeo

Calypso Quinn. An unusual name for an unusual girl. Snowy-white hair, sharp gray eyes, but a soul as dark as night. She didn't like to share things with other people, much less socialize. People would whisper about her, recoiling back from her as she walked through the town of Necro. Necro isn't its official name, of course. It's the reputation of the town that gave it the name "Necro." Necromancy is the art of commanding the dead. And Necro has housed a long bloodline of necromancers. The Quinns. Yes, *that* Quinn. Calypso is the only non-necromancer in her family. The power she has is unlike anything else.

She used it once in her life to protect herself from the claws of death. Hades had sent a pack of hellhounds to bring Calypso to her rightful throne. Being Hades's daughter wasn't an easy job. Especially not with people dying left and right.

"Calypso! Come, darling, come home," he whispered, mist surrounding her body. Calypso didn't so much as shiver. It was horrifying, the amount of control she had over the God of the Underworld. He was known to be ruthless, a dictator at his finest. But according to the rumors, the murmurs of the streets, Hades was a newborn puppy compared to his daughter. She was the reason Persephone left him, the reason Zeus acknowledged him, the reason Hera wanted him dead.

Calypso groaned, inwardly and out. She had grown tired of hearing her insolent father whine about her absence. She had shown him how much more powerful she was, how he shouldn't have threatened her with the hellhounds. Yet still, he pestered her with his requests, and still, he boasted about how "independent" she was. Hades. The God of being a brat. It wasn't every day you get to see the Goddess of Cards in all her deathly glory. Many times she had visited her father, allowed him to start a conversation with her. It almost always ended up in her throwing him into the River Styx. She had Polaroids to prove it. Not that she could show anyone. To the people of Necro, she was just the odd one out. The necro that never was. What a joy it would be to announce that she was adopted. That she was the Goddess of Cards. The one Goddess that didn't give. The one who only took lives and never gave anything in return. The first time Calypso had heard these rumors about the Goddess of Cards, she had snorted so hard that milk came out of her nose. She had laughed, a husky sound, one that her "parents" would deem unladylike. Not that she cared.

Of course, she cared. The only person she ever wanted approval from was her mentor. Her father. Scott Quinn. Whenever he so much as nodded in approval, Calypso would glow with happiness. This didn't happen often, as Scott was normally in Canada, away from her and her mother in Britain. Many people idolized Scott Quinn, Calypso being one of them. But those people never so much as glanced Calypso's way. They would only sniff in disgust.

"How could a prestigious man like Scott ever produce an unearthly creature like *her*?" they'd say, turning their noses up like the snobs that they were.

Calypso would have to cover her mouth in an attempt to hide her grin. Unearthly was right. If only they knew how close they were to striking the nail on its head. Ah, now the blissfully sweet time came to visit her "favorite" person in the world. In truth, she'd do anything to get out of visiting Hades. Even spend the day with Aphrodite. Actually, no. Nothing was worth spending time with Aphrodite. She was a menace disguised as love. Calypso shivered at that thought alone.

A few seconds passed by, and a black shadow surrounded Calypso greedily, practically sucking her into hell. What really was ten seconds felt like an eternity. Calypso opened her eyes and looked around the fiery room. Hades was nowhere to be seen. She craned her neck slowly to the side, looking pointedly at the River Styx.

"Father?" she called, cupping her mouth with both of her hands, her voice echoing in the room.

"Who are you looking for, girl?" a low voice asked, calloused hands gripping Calypso's wrists, acting as handcuffs.

Calypso flicked a finger, and a card flew out of her pocket, cutting her attacker's hands. She heard him curse in Greek, and a split second later, she was free. She spun around, moving her fingers quickly, a deck of cards dancing in rhythm with the movement of her hands. In that same second, fifty-two cards ended up pointing directly at the man's neck, head, heart, and stomach, all sharpened to a point where a single swipe across the skin could leave a scar.

Calypso tilted her head toward the side, inspecting the man in front of her. He was young, there was no doubt about it, but there was a strange aura around him, an aura that screamed Apollo. His hair was a mix of platinum blond and just plain blond, cropped to just above his ear. His eyes held mischief amid an ocean of blue. He wore a plain white V-neck shirt, accompanied with black ripped jeans. She narrowed her eyes. This wasn't Apollo. In fact, she'd never seen this man before. So the only other option was that he was a demigod. Calypso scoffed; she couldn't believe that she had wasted her time scanning for a threat. Demigods were lower class, lower than centaurs. At least, that's what her father said. Calypso herself believed that demigods were just below Gods and Goddesses. The man in front of her noticed her looking at him and flashed her a boyish grin. Calypso rolled her eyes, flicking a finger, leaving only one card pointed at his neck. She walked casually over to the River Styx and peered inside, looking around with lips clamped together.

"Girl, don't! If you fall, you're going to *die!*" the man, ahem, the *boy* warned, urgency in his words.

Calypso's eyes couldn't have rolled farther. Was this boy dumb, or did he not look at her face properly? She looked so much like her father that Hera hated her just as much. Just to make him panic, she stepped inside, both her feet covered by the acidic water. She turned back, face full of unsaid expectations. The boy's mouth was wide open, and it seemed to drop even farther as he took in her face.

"Callie?" the boy murmured, and the cave carried his words all the way to her ears.

Her eyes widened. No one had called her that in six years. There had been only one boy who called her by that nickname.

"Eli?" Calypso whispered, tears forming at the sides of her eyes. Elijah Collins, her childhood best friend. He had left without warning, never even bothering to say goodbye.

Eli's head shot up, a smile forming at his lips. The card dropped to the floor, and he ran straight at her. Calypso did the same. His arms wrapped around her, engulfing her in a warm hug, a hug that she had stopped longing for five years ago.

This felt like home.

Fourteen years later

"Mommy!" Haven called, her little arms clasping around Calypso's leg.

At the young age of seven, Haven was already learning to control her powers. Unlike her mother, she could speak to animals. Like her mother, she strongly disliked Hades.

A bark sounded not too far away from the pair, a low male laugh following shortly after.

"Hello, Haven!" Elijah cooed, his smile dropping into mock dismay as little Haven ran straight past her father, just to cuddle with Ollie, the husky pup Haven had bonded with.

Calypso let out a laugh, her face glowing with joy. Elijah's face softened, and as he walked over to the mother of his child, he hugged her, just as he had fourteen years ago. She melted into his embrace, nestling her head into his shoulder. He placed

Through Their Lenses

a soft kiss on the top of her head, and they both looked at Haven. They smiled at the sight of their daughter playing with Ollie, barking and laughing together. It confused them since they didn't have a single clue as to what they were talking about, but as long as Haven was happy, they were too. Right now, life was as perfect as it could get. And Calypso intended to make it stay that way.

Watch Out!

Quimby Owens

I clearly remember the screech and the screams, the shattering glass, then the blackout.

"Macy, do you have a water bottle?"

"Mom, I know!" I called back.

She was nervous for me because if I did well, the program I'm a part of would submit my scores to a ton of Ivy League schools, which could possibly get me a scholarship. But I wasn't nervous. I knew everything I needed to know.

"Wait, Macy! Do you have a book to read if you finish early?"

I went into the kitchen, pulled *Sense and Sensibility* out of my packed drawstring bag, and plopped it on the counter.

"Okay. I'm sorry, Mace. I'm just excited for you!" she said.

I smiled, shoveling the rest of my half-eaten Raisin Bran into my mouth.

A voice behind me swooped in out of nowhere, "Ooh, my baby girl!" Suddenly I was scooped up off my stool and swung around. I giggled and squealed, and Dad put me down in front of him. I looked up into his light blue eyes—the same color as mine.

"How're you feeling, kiddo?"

"Really excited!" I grinned.

"I'm so proud of you! You're going to do really well. I'll be there to pick you up afterward, and—" He broke off, looked up at Mom, leaned closer to me, and whispered, "We can get ice cream sundaes."

I gasped. "Really?!"

"Shh! Don't let your mother know!" He winked at me.

Mom rolled her eyes, grinning in spite of herself.

Through Their Lenses

"I'm kidding. If she can, I'll bring her along to pick you up."

"We're both very proud of you," Mom added, ushering me out of the house. "Let's get in the car. Do you have a water bottle?" she asked (again).

"Of course she does, Momma! Don't worry about our little cynosure," Dad consoled.

I laughed at Dad, who tried to keep up with my college vocabulary (but rarely succeeded). I said bye to him, got in the car, and started my pretest breathing technique.

You see, when I was a baby, my parents took me everywhere. Parks, basketball courts, churches, offices, libraries, shopping malls, ice-cream shops, everywhere they could. I eventually learned that the patterns in the sounds they were making were called words. I was amazed!

By two years old, I was talking in run-on sentences, then run-on paragraphs. It was time for me to conquer my next frontier—numbers. I used my parents to get this tricky concept under my belt. If they placed a bowl of blueberries in front of me, I would say, "How many?" They would smile and count my blueberries for me. That was the beginning of my math education.

Eventually, that word absorption led to little stories, then essays, then theses. Counting blueberries led me to advanced calculus and trigonometry. My parents have supported me through it all, but they were concerned that I wasn't finding "my kind of people." They enrolled me in a program that gives opportunities (like the ACT) to gifted kids. These kinds of programs are great because they give me friends, kids my age, kids with my kind of brain. We're a really tight-knit community because there aren't many of us.

We arrived at the testing center. I'm really not nervous. Really.

Mom smiles at me, and I know she gets it. She always does.

"Hi, what's your name?" asked the check-in lady. Her name tag said her name was Amira.

"Macy Evans," I told her, handing her my papers.

"Room 177, right across the hall." She smiled, pointing me to the room.

"Thank you," I said politely.

I sat down at my desk in Room 177 and waited patiently for the instructor.

He explained the test, then said, "You may begin."

"How'd it go, Macy?" Dad asked as he opened the car door for me.

"Pretty good, I think. Some of the science questions were bizarre."

We walked out into the parking lot. Mom, whose boss let her off early, opened the car door for me. I thanked her and slid in.

"Yikes, my brain is fried," I sighed, rubbing my forehead. I'd gotten a headache from the fluorescent lights in the testing room.

"Luckily, we have cold ice-cream sundaes to cool it down."

I grinned.

We pulled out of the parking lot and drove to the ice-cream shop.

I grabbed both of their hands and skipped into the Frozen Spoon. I made a *masterpiece* of a sundae, and we grabbed a table outside, soaking up the beautiful crisp day.

I shoved my spoon into the sugary tower and took my first heavenly bite.

"Macy, we have something we want to tell you. We've been wanting to talk to you about this for a while," Mom announced.

Dad reached over and put his hand on hers.

"You're going to have a sister soon."

I choked on my whipped cream.

"You're telling the truth?!" I gasped, barely believing it. Mom laughed and nodded. I rushed into her arms.

"Oh, I'm *so ecstatic*! Congratulations! I can't *wait*!" I squealed.

We ate the rest of the ice cream, talking and laughing and celebrating.

We got in the car, full and happy. I literally bounced in my seat from excitement. Dad pulled out of the parking lot.

"Watch out!" Mom yelled.

The screech and the screams, the shattering glass, then the blackout.

Lazy, foggy thoughts floated through my head. Sometimes I thought of random math problems to pass the time. I thought about what I would write about in my wrap-up book report once I'd finished *Sense and Sensibility*. Three days later, I woke up and opened my eyes.

There was a cast on my leg, a brace on my back, and a heavy bandage turban around my head.

Blazingly white fluorescent lights made me squint to see what was around me. My first reaction to these lights was that I would get headaches from them.

It took me a while to really wake up, about a day in total. Eventually, the doctors noticed. When they did, they started rushing around me, poking and prodding and squeezing and spouting a bunch of medical nonsense.

"Excuse me, where am I?" I croaked. All of the anxious thoughts (which had been graciously held off while I was sleeping) rushed into my mind.

The doctor, a tall blonde woman, was the first to respond to my question. "Miss Macy, you were in a car crash. Luckily all of your injuries are minor. Your seat belt worked impressively well, and the impact didn't affect the back seat too much."

She specified the back seat.

"Where are Mom and Dad?"

The doctor froze. She took a deep breath and glanced at the nurse beside her. He looked away hastily.

"No," I stated. It couldn't have happened. "No, don't tell me. Don't tell me! *Don't tell me!*" I screamed, pushing away what I now knew had happened.

My parents were dead. My unborn sister was dead. I was alone.

Tears streamed down my face but were stopped by my bandages. There they sat, on my chin, as though I would never escape the grief that had seized me by its dark hand.

My parents are dead. I am alone.

I am alone in a big, big world.

Five years, two months, six days, and twenty-three minutes later

"Macy, do you have a water bottle?" Amira asks.

"Affirmative, captain!" I chant back.

After a few weeks in the hospital and a couple of agonizing months bouncing around different houses, Amira brought me home. It was tense and awkward for a while. But after the ice broke, we became the best of friends. In spite of all that, I've been ready to go to college for a while.

"Everything else loaded up?" she asks.

"You know it!" I say cheerfully.

"C'mon, Mace-Ace! Princeton awaits," she announces, opening the front door.

"Yeah, aren't *you* glad? *You* don't have to pay because *I* got a full scholarship."

"Okay, you just like taunting me with your 'full scholarship' because you know that *I'm* still paying off my student debt," she responds, putting her hands on her hips.

"Thirty-nine, Amira. You're thirty-nine," I say, shaking my head incredulously. "You know, *some* people just don't have the intellectual power that I do," I add, linking her arm through mine and skipping out the door.

She rolls her eyes. I grin and pile all my stuff into the bed of her truck. She slides in the driver's seat and I take shotgun. I'd wanted to drive myself to Princeton because of the symbolism—me, taking the wheel of my life! But she insisted that she wanted to drive, as a favor to me, starting my adult life. Eventually, I relented. I'm excited about living at college, and I'm glad Amira is supportive.

The world opens itself up to me as Amira and I drive up to Princeton. I'm ready for whatever life throws at me!

"Watch out!"

The Raccoon and the Cactus

August Watson

It came to the raccoon's attention that it was slowly wandering through a withered, vacant desert. What also struck the raccoon was that it was exceedingly thirsty. These were elementary thoughts, but important ones. These were thoughts about existence, about survival.

The raccoon knew little about the anatomy of the world and had little common sense, but in this situation, it did know one phenomenon of the earth. Cacti provide water. The raccoon had little idea as to why this fact was part of its weak intellect, but as this thought came into the raccoon's mind, it was immediately overwhelmed by the idea. It became a driving thought to the raccoon, and that was all that it could focus on for the time being.

The raccoon continued to trudge along the dry desert landscape, shrouded by the magnificent golden sunlight. The heat from the light felt as if it seared the raccoon's coat and boiled its skin down to nothingness. Time passed as slowly as ever. To the raccoon, seconds felt like minutes, and minutes felt like hours.

The raccoon had never experienced sensations like these before and regretted coming to the desert in the first place.

After more thought, the raccoon realized that it didn't know how it had gotten to this desert. The days before had blurred together, making the raccoon's memory a fuzzy mess. Soon the feeling of regret passed out of the raccoon's head as it mustered up its energy to continue through the arid landscape in search of the water it needed to survive.

On the raccoon went, its fatigue increasing greatly. The raccoon had now fully receded into its mind. Its surveillance levels plummeted, as it fought to keep its eyes open. The raccoon's feet had become inflamed and blistered, causing it to slow down by an even larger degree than previously. The raccoon feared it might not make it to water in time.

Now it had become the evening, and the sun's light weakened, giving the raccoon a slight break from its recent trepidation. As the sun began to dip below the horizon, its deep purple and red light fell upon a cactus, standing tall in the vast, tranquil, twilight desert. The raccoon did not see this cactus, its only hope at being liberated from the torture of nature. For maybe the treacherous part of the raccoon's escapade could have been joyously concluded if it had laid eyes upon the cactus. But now the opportunity had perished, for the sun had gone beyond the horizon, and the desert had become opaque.

The raccoon came to a stop and fretted about what would happen next. When it could not come up with a plan, or merely an idea, it commanded itself to push through, and obtain the last drops of vigor from within. That the raccoon did, and again it began to tramp through the desert, but only this time, blindly.

The raccoon felt as if its whole body was completely numbed, as if it was floating over the ground. It seemed to the raccoon that it was in a bubble, all of its senses muted, and its mind reeling in the darkness.

Suddenly the raccoon stopped dead and felt a searing pain in its cheek. Something had pricked it, something of adequate size too. Cacti had spikes and were reasonably sized, and the raccoon knew these things. Indubitably it was a cactus.

By some small sliver of a chance, the raccoon had grasped a thread of luck, and now it had to hold on to it. The raccoon dislodged the cactus spike from its cheek and snapped it off the cactus, invigorated at the thought of getting water.

"Not so fast, *traveler*," sneered the cactus, seeming offended. "You want my water I presume?" The raccoon didn't dare to answer the question. "It may prove to be a difficult task." The cactus waited, as if expecting a response. The raccoon kept its mouth shut.

"I have spikes as sharp as knives, but a weakness lies upon my skin. If you are careful you might reach your prize, your water that you so desperately require. One of us will perish at the end of this cunning interplay. You will have to make your decision, *traveler*. So what do you say, and what will you do?" the cactus said, concluding its rant.

Out of all of the things that could have happened, the raccoon was least expecting this. It was overwhelmed by this unexpected monologue and greatly taken aback. The raccoon was annoyed and angered by the cactus's purposeful circumlocution and riddles. The raccoon thought about what was happening, and it had no clear explanation for it. The raccoon knew that it needed water, and that it would die if it did not get it. The cactus was the problem; the thing that was supposed to save it could end up doing the exact opposite.

The raccoon fought with its reflexes, finally stumbling forward toward the cactus. It then injected its sharp claws into a break in between its spikes. A waterlike juice seeped out of the puncture, soothing the raccoon's irritated pads.

"I see you have made your decision," the cactus exclaimed grimly, its attitude suddenly changing. The raccoon was dismayed by this formidable comment, for it was at war with its own mind, the thing that had gotten it to this point. It withdrew its claw from the cactus skin. The raccoon thought of the water and what came with it, the ceasing of pain, its thirst being finally quenched. These thoughts enticed the raccoon's mind, making its tongue tingle with anticipation.

To the raccoon, the situation was getting unendurable. If it could not decide soon, it was sure that it would not last very long. The situation was ambiguous to the raccoon, and that is why it had such difficulty deciding what to do. This situation was a hindrance to the process of survival.

Suddenly the raccoon made an abrupt decision. It thrust its claw into the now dried puncture in the cactus, tearing the skin apart. The hole grew larger and larger, and the raccoon's

Through Their Lenses

thirst lessened. The raccoon became fanatical about getting the water, as its mind craved it more and more.

In a short amount of time, the raccoon had decimated the entire cactus and deprived it of nearly all of its water. As the cactus fell to the ground, the raccoon heard an almost inaudible sigh come from the frail, broken figure. The raccoon meandered away, as if nothing had ever happened.

As dawn came upon the barren landscape, the raccoon collapsed onto the dry earthen desert floor, and its heart's beating ceased. For its mouth was as dry as ever, and the silhouette of the dismantled cactus was no more. The raccoon's mind had led itself to its own demise, digging itself into a hole that was far too deep to escape.

Determination

Sarah Serena Thompson

Warsaw, Poland
1941

I rushed through the streets, clutching the stolen bread. The German soldiers were after me. But I could escape. Through cracks, through alleys, or in between people, the places to escape were endless for a small girl like me.

I tore through the streets like a crazed hen. People leaned out their windows to look at me. I glanced behind my shoulder. The soldiers were still chasing me. I knew I must evacuate their sight before they used their guns.

I came to a halt for a millisecond, and before me lay two choices of escape. I could go down an alleyway that ended up in a dead end and look for a crevice to hide in, or I could dodge vehicles and people that were venturing along the busy street.

I made my choice.

I ran into the busy street.

The soldiers continued to shout at me as I hurled myself into people. I pushed past them as quickly as I could. There were many tanks roaming through our once beautiful streets. I had to watch out for them. They were large, heavy, and could easily crush anyone.

I dodged fruit carts, people, more people, and soldiers. I quickly glanced over my shoulder to see if I was still being chased. To my dismay, they were still following me. I reached the end of the street and ran down a cramped alleyway, knocking things over as I went. People were yelling at me right and left and trying to grab me and my bread. I clutched it tighter and continued running.

I ran past several of my mother's friends who summoned me to them, but I did not obey. I am an orphan now. I have no elders to obey.

The German officers yelled at me to stop many times. In fact, everyone was yelling at me, saying various things. But I blocked everyone out. I heard nothing but a slight buzzing.

I could tell that I was losing the officers; they were slowing down and panting. I was surprised they lasted that long. I ran for a few more streets, and then stopped and looked behind me. I had lost them; they were no longer following me.

I sat down on the curb and bit into the soft, chewy bread. It was still warm from the oven. I devoured it. Then I bit into the apple that I had in my pocket. I took a few deep breaths and reminisced about the fresh apples that we had once had. The new ones were dry and mealy. I remembered the warm, gooey apple pies my mother used to bake. Times were better then.

While I ate the last few bites of my bread, I thought about the beautiful taste of butter. The Nazi soldiers had regulated all the butter. Regulated, meaning they had banned it.

I sat watching people walk by me for a few minutes. Then I heard the sound of voices speaking in German. I recognized the voices. They were coming closer to me.

I realized a second too late.

The soldiers that chased me earlier had turned the street corner and now faced me.

I froze.

They froze.

The people around us froze.

I quickly came to my senses and bolted.

So off we went. They were chasing me, but faster this time. The soldiers had rested. This was an unfair battle.

People were yelling and running out of the way. The soldiers were yelling at me to stop.

And then it happened.

In slow motion, I tripped and fell. I felt as if I could not move a single muscle. They were two steps away from me. I felt trapped, like a bear in a cage. My brain told my muscles to do something, anything at all. But I could not.

Then I felt myself being dragged away.

I told myself that I could not go like this. I had to do something. I could not let them win.

My muscles spasmed, and I squirmed and writhed. I felt as if I was wrestling in honey. Everything was still in slow motion. I kicked one of the soldier's arms, and he let go of my leg. The crowd yelled. I jumped up and ran, faster than I had ever run before.

The Mystery of the Horrible Smell
Valerie Menke

"Yes!"

It was the day of my birthday party. I had just hopped out of bed and stumbled down the stairs, a little dizzy from getting up too fast. I was in the kitchen about to pour myself a nice, big bowl of cereal, but stopped myself. My dog, Ginger, was scratching at the door. I let her in, and she scurried to the mudroom and lay on her bed. I opened the refrigerator to grab the milk when something strange happened.

A funny smell flowed through the air. It was a funky smell and very faint at first. Then I did something I very much regret.

I took a big sniff and...ew!

I thought I was going to barf. Oh, that terrible, horrible smell! I dashed sideways, headed for the back door nearly knocking over my mom's favorite coffee cup left out from the day before. The door swung open, and I leaped into the grass. I landed on my butt, breathing heavily, trying to catch my breath from racing around the kitchen and into the grass. Yes, the smell was that bad. You know the smell of rotten eggs, stinky socks, throw up, or maybe roadkill? Yeah, I know, disgusting.

After catching my breath, I was curious what that horrible smell was, and knowing I needed to figure that out before my party started, I had to go back inside. So I made a plan. I went around the back of the house and came to the front door. I decided to check with my mom first to see if she knew what was causing the smell, so I slowly pushed the door open and stepped in.

I didn't forget to plug my nose.

The smell was much stronger now and seeping outside the kitchen. I headed up the stairs to the second floor, and on the way to my mom's room, I bumped into my oldest sister.

"Hey," I said, holding my nose.

After sneezing, my sister replied, "Good morning." She had been fighting a cold. As we walked past each other, her eyebrows raised probably because I was holding my nose. I almost forgot to tell her about the horrible smell.

"Wait!"

She spun around and asked, "What?"

"You don't want to go down there. Something smells really bad. So bad I almost barfed. I'm trying to figure out what it is before the party starts, but I don't know yet."

"Well, it can't be that bad."

"Trust me, it's bad. If you don't believe me, that's fine, but don't say I didn't warn you."

She chuckled and started down the stairs anyway.

I continued to my mom's room, on a mission. "Mom, what's that horrible smell downstairs?"

"I haven't been downstairs yet, but maybe it's your sister's volleyball kneepads?"

I darted to my other sister's room where she was sleeping and pounced on the side of her bed. She flew out and onto the ground.

Startled, she screamed, "Bananas!"

"Why did you scream bananas?"

"Because I was dreaming about bananas."

Normally I would have laughed at that, but this was no laughing matter. This was serious. What if it got worse and ruined my party? I asked my sister, "Where are your kneepads?"

"Over there." She pointed to the center of her room where the pile of all her dirty clothes were. As smelly as the pile was, it wasn't the scent I'd picked up earlier.

The rumble of the garage door gave me an idea. Dad was home from his bike ride around the lake! Maybe he knew what was going on. I hurried through the hallway and down the stairs. I missed two steps and tumbled down the rest and landed on my face.

Dad helped me up. "Are you okay?"

"No! There's a horrible smell and it's coming from…"

"Sorry, I just got back from a bike ride."

"It's not you. It smells like…burned rubber. Plus, you weren't here when it started. But we have to figure it out. My party starts in two hours!" I imagined my friends arriving and holding their noses. Nobody would want to play any party games or eat cake.

I took him to the kitchen where my oldest sister was eating her waffle.

"How could you be eating at a time like this?" I asked her.

She shrugged and said, "I have a cold, remember? I can't smell anything."

It was one time I wished I was sick.

"Could it be coming from the dryer?" Mom said, growing concerned.

Dad went into the mudroom to check. "No, there's no smell coming from the dryer, but I definitely smell something."

I kneeled down to pet Ginger as Dad kept looking around. When I touched her head, her normally soft, curly fur was damp and sticky. I leaned over and took a big whiff.

"Yuck!" I jumped away from Ginger and bumped into my oldest sister who was standing in the doorway. Mom was there too.

We all looked at each other, and at that very moment, it hit us at the same time. We knew where the horrible smell was coming from…

IT WAS GINGER.

She'd been skunked!!!

"Dad, you let her out! You are the culprit," I announced.

"I think the skunk was the culprit," Dad said.

Ginger got five baths in tomato juice from a professional tomato juice bather (also known as Dad). Mom turned on fans and opened windows, and we decided to move the party outside. My middle sister canceled on her friends coming over. My oldest sister laughed since she didn't smell anything.

And I lay on the couch, crossing my arms over my chest, admiring how I had accomplished my mission.

The case was solved.

I told my family that from now on we would let Ginger out on a leash. I felt relieved that my friends would be able to enjoy the party like we'd planned. Maybe I could solve another case. I wondered what.

I'd be our family detective. I'd never give up, no matter what obstacles were in my way.

Even if they were stinky.

Through Their Lenses

About Lune Spark Books

Lune Spark Books aims to encourage children to engage in creating writing. We work with parents and young writers to promote creative fiction writing to help identify talent. We run annual competitions and creative writing classes and publish short stories by the young writers. For more details, visit us at http://lunespark.com/youngwriters/.

For the details of the contest or to enroll in the contest, please visit us at
http://lunespark.com/youngwriters/storycontest/.

Follow us on social media to keep up with the latest updates:
https://www.facebook.com/youngwriterscontest/
https://twitter.com/LuneSparkLLC

Other Anthologies by Lune Spark

A Window to Young Minds *(Age: 10+ years)*
This book is the first of the Lune Spark Short Story Contest's yearly anthologies and includes twenty-five award-winning short stories by young writers.

The Emotional Embodiment of Stars *(Age: 13+ years)*
Wonderfully wide-ranging, original, and enjoyable, this outstanding collection features twenty-seven short stories like *Mortimer*, in which an unwanted guest secretly follows a family through their heartbreaking sorrows.

Speaking Up for Each Other *(Age: 10+ years)*
Wonderfully wide-ranging, original, and enjoyable, this outstanding collection features twenty-four short stories like That Glowing Penny, in which a helpless girl has to live in fear of her own family.

Stained Glass Myths *(Age: 13+ years)*
A collection of twenty-eight award-winning stories by young adults. These stories encompass a wide range of genres, inviting readers to explore a wealth of important themes passionately crafted by these young writers— from a teenager going down memory lane after a tragic event at her school to a Jewish boy who writes letters to his older sister who's been taken to Auschwitz.

Just One More *(Age: 10+ years)*
A collection of twenty-nine award-winning short stories by middle grade children. These stories encompass a wide range of genres, inviting readers to explore a wealth of important themes passionately crafted by these young writers—from a beautiful dragon called

Ephyral giving up her freedom to save her entire species to a fifteen-year-old girl named Louisa Brixham dealing with her brother being accused of a crime she committed.

Seasons of Grief *(Age: 13+ years)*

Seasons of Grief is a collection of twenty-seven award-winning stories by teens. These stories encompass a wide range of genres, inviting readers to explore a wealth of important themes passionately crafted by these young writers: from a middle-aged woman suffering losses in the heart of Nazi Germany to a teen finding it hard to cope with the loss of a close friend.

Made in the USA
Columbia, SC
18 May 2023